Praise for Donna Alward's
Sold to the Highest Bidder

"a remarkable story...The magnetic chemistry between Ella and Dev pulses through each page..."

~ *SingleTitles.com*

Look for these titles by
Donna Alward

Now Available:

The Girl Most Likely

Almost A Family

Breathe

Sold to the Highest Bidder

Donna Alward

SAMHAIN
PUBLISHING

Samhain Publishing, Ltd.
577 Mulberry Street, Suite 1520
Macon, GA 31201
www.samhainpublishing.com

Editing by Heidi Moore
Cover by Kanaxa

First Samhain Publishing, Ltd. electronic publication: April 2010
First Samhain Publishing, Ltd. print publication: February 2011

Dedication

To my readers, who make this job such a joy.

Chapter One

Smoke, whiskey and old grease.

Ella's delicate nostrils flared, assimilating it all within a step inside Ruby Shoes Saloon. The neon sign above the bar glared out a pair of crimson shoes with one stiletto heel unlit. The noise was deafening. Lynyrd Skynyrd blared from speakers on either side of what was normally a huge dance floor. Seeing the way a biker's eyes were following the gyrations of a woman in a red mini-skirt, Ella curled her lip. She was beginning to see that the bar was the catwalk for a meat market. Now the dance floor was extended into some sort of makeshift stage, a long black runner rolled down the center of it.

Around her, shouts mingled with the slamming down of shot glasses. Catcalls echoed as one leggy brunette leaned over the pool table. Ella straightened her black pencil skirt and ran a hand over her smooth twist of carefully tinted blonde hair. She pushed away the dark sense of déjà vu.

Damn. She never thought she'd be here again.

She edged her way over to the bar while several pairs of eyes stared at her. She should have known better than to wear work dress here. She stuck out like a sore thumb in her tidy skirt and blouse. Her only hope was that if she did see someone she knew, they wouldn't recognize her. She looked as much like a stranger as she felt, and that was exactly how she wanted it.

The last thing she needed was for anyone to put two and two together and remember her.

Skynyrd changed to the Steve Miller Band and she hid a smile. They were still playing the same music now as they had over twelve years ago. The bar was still battered and scarred and the glasses old and foggy from too many washings. She bit her lip and stepped up to the walnut-colored counter. She just had to get through this night. An hour, that was all. After that she could check into her hotel. Then tomorrow she'd see Dev and clear up the small matter of their legal issues. She raised a finger and thanked the Lord she didn't recognize the bartender.

"White wine. Whatever you've got's fine." The bartender angled a wry eyebrow in her direction and she looked away. Ruby's certainly wasn't the trendy martini bar she was used to frequenting. And to think that many years ago she'd been nervous wondering if she was going to be IDed at Ruby's doors. Now she was simply wondering if ordering a house white was living a little too dangerously.

Ha, living dangerously. Her thoughts immediately turned to Dev and a shiver of nervousness skittered up her spine. He had to have changed in the years since she'd seen him. At eighteen he'd already been grown, sure of himself and oh so sexy. She hadn't been able to resist him. For a brief moment she wondered if she should have ordered something stronger for fortification. Just the thought of seeing Dev tomorrow made her hands sweat. Twelve years of silence made a girl wonder. What was he doing? How would he look? And how would she react seeing the man to whom she'd willingly given her innocence, not to mention her heart?

No, it would be fine. She wasn't a love-struck girl anymore, full of hormones and dreams and willing to take risks. That bubble of idealism had been popped.

She slid the bartender a bill and set her lips. Worrying about it also made her feel like the world's biggest coward, and she hated that. But right now she had a job to do. She had to remember that. She pushed her thoughts about Devin to the side. She'd deal with him later.

An emcee stood at the mic and raised his hands for quiet. Someone turned down the music. Good Lord, was that Scooter Brown at the mic? He tilted his battered cowboy hat back on his head as he leaned into the microphone. It *was* Scooter, who'd run the garage out on the highway for as long as she could remember. Ella sipped her wine and shuddered. She shouldn't have taken the risk on the chardonnay. Whiskey would have been much safer.

"Well now. I see everyone's greased their wheels...thank you. Betty Tucker thanks you too." Scooter nodded at the people now gravitating to the stage. "We're sure glad you showed up to the benefit tonight. We all want Betty on the mend as soon as possible. 'Course the insurance companies couldn't give a good damn—"

Someone in the audience coughed. Ella put down her wine and fished into her purse for a pen. She was here to work. It would do to remember that.

"Right, right." Scooter cleared his throat loudly. "Well, let's get on with our show. Now the truth is the best thing to come out of Backwards Gulch is its stock. And we ain't talking the bovine or equine type." Scooter laughed uproariously at his own joke while several whistles and whoops erupted. "No, sir," he drawled. "Tonight Ruby Shoes is holding its first ever bachelor auction."

Oh, no. Ella's mouth almost dropped open before she resolutely clamped her lips together again. A bachelor auction? Charlie Donovan wouldn't have sent her here. To *this*. She'd been begging for a big story for ages but had remained stuck in Lifestyles for what seemed like forever. Donovan had pitched the charity benefit and Amy had lifted her hand for her, the traitor. Damn that Amy—she called herself a best friend but she had some answering to do. She was the only one in Ella's life that knew Durango was *home*. And that Devin McQuade was unfinished business.

If Ella wanted a promotion—if she wanted the limelight— she couldn't afford to let Dev be a skeleton in her proverbial closet. She'd known it for years. Now her chance was so close she could taste it, and Devin McQuade was one annoying albatross hanging around her neck. She poised her pen over her notebook. Somehow she'd turn this small-time auction into a major story—it was all a matter of finding the right angle and exploiting it. It would put her one more rung up the ladder of her career. Then she'd put Devin behind her once and for all. The albatross was getting heavy after all these years.

"So let's get on with the auction!" Scooter's voice boomed through the speakers. More whistles pierced the air as ladies jostled for a position at the front of the stage. Ella turned up her nose. This sure as hell explained the larger than normal proportion of females to males tonight.

"Miss Carbunckle here is gonna read out the intros, if you will. And I'm going to do the bidding. Remember, ladies, this is for a good cause. Betty's chemo ain't comin' cheap, and this is your chance to help out a neighbor."

Ella swallowed more wine, and quickly. She flipped to a clean page in her notebook, knowing she could scribble faster than type into her PDA. Later, in her hotel room, she'd transpose everything into her laptop. She had to remember why she was really here. To get the scoop on a benefit for Betty Tucker. And if Ella had her way, tonight's auction was only the tip of the iceberg. This was one measly step in the big story—

blowing the HMO to pieces. She just had to ask the right questions.

Ruby Shoes, on the outskirts of Durango, was where everyone in Backwards Gulch went to tie one on or simply kill a Friday night. And if that was the case...a sudden thought struck. *Everyone.* How many of the bachelors would she actually *know*? How many would remember her? Heat rose in her face at the very idea, and she slid farther back into a corner where she could get a good view and attempt to remain inconspicuous.

"First up for bid is Jason O'Leary."

Lewd music played from the speakers and Ella smothered a laugh. Jason O'Leary had been the fat kid two years behind her in school. But as he came through the makeshift curtain in the back, her mouth clamped shut. Jason wasn't the fat kid anymore. Nope. He was actually looking good—really good—in what was most of a fireman's uniform. At least the pants. The suspenders lay flat against a very tanned and muscled torso. Miss Carbunckle gave the short bio as he walked to the end of the catwalk. And then the bidding began.

Ella put her wine glass down on a nearby table and jotted down impressions. A trip down memory lane wasn't why she was here, thank God. She was smart enough to know there was a more to it than a bunch of blue-collar buddies raising a few grand to help a neighbor. Charlie wouldn't have sent any of his reporters here for a simple auction. As the bidding went higher, she watched as Jason took a slightly awkward turn on the stage. Her story was only a small part. But this time, she'd angle it right and get a piece of the pie. And get the hell out of the Lifestyles section for good.

She jotted down notes, satisfied with her beginning. It just so happened that the trip was convenient, that's all. Divorce papers currently sat on the front seat of her rented Miata in a lovely, virtually indestructible Tyvek envelope. Getting her marriage officially over with was merely a happy by-product of an assignment, killing two birds with one stone. She'd sent papers to Dev several times over the years, and they just kept coming back to her. Without a signature. The one benefit of coming to Durango was having the opportunity to get Devin to sign them. No matter what. Tonight the story, tomorrow the divorce. And before she knew it her life would finally be on the path she wanted. Free and clear of any of the ties holding her back.

Ella turned her attention back to the auction. The bidding got fast and furious as the hour wore on, and she started to relax. No one had recognized her yet. She ordered a soft drink, paying and putting the change in the Betty Tucker tip bucket. Her pen flew over her notepad. Betty was loved by her neighbors, that was obvious. One by one, the bachelors were auctioned off—the winners getting forty-eight hours of beck-and-call service. She smiled behind a finger as she watched some of the women lead off their winnings. It took a brave man to agree to such an arrangement.

"Ella? Ella McQuade?"

Her head snapped around. No one called her that. Ever. A vision in jeans and a slightly too-tight top was bearing down on her. Jesus. Tanya Bryan. Of all the luck. Damn, having Tanya recognize her meant that within the hour Dev would know she was in town. The element of surprise would be shot. His sister, for God's sake. She cursed under her breath before pasting on a smile.

"Hey, Tanya, how're you?" Her stomach twisted. The chardonnay-in-a-box was coming back to bite her. She held her fake smile at the older, rounder version of the woman who happened to be her sister-in-law.

14

"Never thought I'd see you back in these parts again. Have you come to bid, Ella?"

Ella ignored the question. "You get a sitter tonight?" She smiled thinly and looked back at the stage.

Tanya smiled, shaking her head so that her ponytail swished on her shoulders. "Hell, no. Julie's damn near thirteen. She's watchin' the other two for a couple of hours. Thought Bob and I would come out and give Betty a hand, you know?"

There was a successful bid and a rowdy cheer rose from the crowd. Ella had missed it though, due to Tanya's distraction. She bit down on her lip in annoyance.

Ella hadn't ever been close to Tanya. She was four years older than Devin and it hadn't been cool to hang out with a baby brother and his girlfriend. Tanya had gone to secretarial school and then worked keeping the books for a company in Silverton until she and Bob got married. It certainly wasn't the life Ella had wanted, but she couldn't help but admire the way Tanya—and the whole community—rallied around a sick woman.

"Yeah, I do know, Tanya." She tucked her notebook away in her bag. The last thing she wanted was questions and prying. She offered a weak smile instead.

"Are you sure you're not biddin', Ella?"

There was something in the other woman's voice that put her on edge. Her fingers played with her pen, clicking and unclicking it as her discomfort grew. Her brow furrowed at Tanya's sly grin but cleared instantly when she realized why Dev's sister was laughing.

Because Scooter said a name and a man walked out on the stage in worn jeans and a long-sleeved navy T. In dusty boots with his hair a sexy study in *who gives a damn*. Her heart pounded and the pen felt slippery in her fingers as she

15

struggled to keep the pasted smile on her face. He was as heart-stoppingly sexy now as he'd been then. Lean where a man needed to be lean, and filled out...exactly where a pair of Levi's should be filled out. He was older. Rougher. The memory of his hands worshiping her skin slid over her. Her breath caught as she wondered if he still had the pair of dents just above his tailbone. She pushed the memory away. It had no place in her life now.

He smiled down at the crowd and her lips parted at the sight of it. And as one of his dimples popped, he turned his head and looked right at her.

Her husband.

Damn.

Devin's smile threatened to falter as their eyes caught. Not the Ella he remembered, but a different one. This Ella had her hair done up and was dressed in fancy clothes and prissy shoes. Still, he'd know her anywhere. The soft curve of her lips, the smoky depth of her eyes. His body flickered to life as that gaze now clashed with his. And... *Oh God.* She was standing with Tanya. Could this night get any worse?

His gaze held hers and he would swear the air sizzled between them, hitting his stomach and settling between his thighs. It had always been this way between them, hot and electric. He'd be a liar to deny it. He was just surprised he reacted as instantly at thirty as he had at sixteen.

Miss Carbunkle read out his bio—the very basic one *he'd* provided, not the promotional claptrap that had recently appeared in *Colorado Entrepreneur.* Thank God. The last thing he needed Ella to hear tonight was the truth about who he'd become. It was bad enough he was offering himself up for sacrifice. He was only doing it for Betty. Never had he expected to see his wife here. But here she was. Honest to God, in the flesh, in Ruby Shoes. At the very moment he was on the bachelor block. And he could tell she was as surprised as he.

So why was she here?

Scooter started the bidding and Dev made his eyes slide away from hers. But he already remembered exactly how she looked. Pencil-thin black skirt and a white blouse that clung to her tidy little figure. One button too many undone...leaving tempting glimpses of the valley between her breasts. Knowing it made his hands itch.

He hadn't been this itchy in a long time. And all it took was one look at Ella. Dammit. He had to think of something else, or his uncomfortable predicament was going to be noticeable. On the stage. One thing he knew for sure...being up here was far worse than any hostile boardroom he'd ever encountered. In a meeting room he was in control. He knew what he was doing. Being auctioned off for his body...that was a whole other issue. Only for Betty would he do such a thing.

He dug deep and turned on the charm, smiling down at the women below as Scooter's calls began to chatter. There was Kate McGrew, the general manager at the Animas River Resort, her dark head among the crowd below. He liked her. He could spend forty-eight fun-filled hours with her and not have to worry about her wanting more than she should. He should know—he'd hired her, and their relationship had always been strictly platonic. *Bid*, his eyes pleaded with her, and then slid back to Ella. Kate's eyes followed, met his again. Kate had been bailing him out of trouble for a long time. She was a friend, that was all. A friend who knew very well the hell he'd been through after Ella left him.

"Two hundred dollars from Katie McGrew!" Scooter called.

Do I have two fifty? Two fifty? Who'll give me two fifty for Devin McQuade?"

His gaze slid to Ella again. She'd gone slightly white and he grinned. Good. Let her see what she'd run away from like her tail was on fire. The sudden rush of resentment didn't surprise him in the least. It just wasn't as frequent now as it had been a decade ago when it had nearly eaten him up inside. He'd moved on. It appeared she had too. He hooked his thumbs in his pockets.

And saw her lift her hand.

"Two fifty! I have two fifty from... Holy hell." Scooter sat his hat back farther on his head and squinted down towards the bar. "That you, Ella? Two fifty from Ella Turner. I'll be damned." Scooter turned expectantly to first Devin and then Katie.

"Three hundred," Katie called out, and Dev threw her a lightning grin of gratitude. God, they'd laugh over this later, over a couple of drinks and maybe a basket of wings.

He didn't know what Ella wanted from him, but he could guess. The cinnamon Tic Tac he'd popped in his mouth seemed to sour. If there was one thing he knew for sure, it was that she wouldn't get it easily. And she definitely wouldn't get it tonight.

"Three fifty," came a call. From his wife. His blood surged. Forty-eight hours with Ella was a whole different thing. In forty-eight hours... There wouldn't be the laughs he'd have with Katie. But in forty-eight hours he could do a bang-up job in showing Ella what she'd discarded. The idea held a certain amount of appeal. It would be no less than she'd done to him.

"Hoooeeee!" Scooter was getting into it now. "This is what I'm talkin' about. Three fifty for Betty Tucker. Don't shy away now, ladies. Rumor has it Dev here's mighty good with his hands. Who'll give me four hundred?"

"Take off your shirt!" came an anonymous call from the

crowd, and laughter followed.

He looked over at Ella. She looked like she was being put through the seven tortures of hell. Maybe she did need a reminder. A flash of memory raced through his brain—of being teenagers and the feel of her fingers touching his chest for the first time. His gaze held her eyes as he fought back embarrassment—as a rule he was not into running around shirtless. She had been the one to walk away, and she'd been the one to ask for a divorce without ever showing her face in Backwards Gulch again. Why? That summer they'd been inseparable, newlywed and unable to get enough of each other.

A flicker of the pain he'd felt at her leaving slashed through him. He knew it was small, he knew it was petty, but he wanted her to get an eyeful of what she'd let get away. Tonight her discomfort was a fringe benefit. Slowly he grabbed the hem of his T-shirt and lifted it over his head while the bar went strangely silent, like a collective group of voyeurs waiting expectantly for what would happen next. Once the shirt was off, he dropped it from one hand to the dusty floor at his feet and saw Ella swallow while the rest of her body was still as a post.

"Four hundred..." said Scooter expectantly.

The nudge broke the spell. The bids came faster from others in the crowd while Dev felt increasingly exposed. "I have five... I have five fifty. Who'll give me six? I have six. Six fifty for Dev here. I have six fifty."

Katie's finger lifted as she smirked. "Seven, Scooter."

God love her. Dev sent a look of thanks in her direction. The girl was good to her friends. And Dev was thankful to be one of them at this moment.

"I have seven hundred...seven hundred going once...twice..."

"Two thousand dollars."

The bar fell silent, except for the big screen in the corner that emitted the hushed sounds of a baseball game. Each head turned towards Ella and Devin saw her flush.

"Two thousand dollars. To Ella Turner."

Dev didn't correct Scooter on the use of her last name. Their marriage was a matter of record but they hadn't lived together long enough to make it practical. For some she was Ella Turner. For him, she'd always be Ella McQuade, and at the moment, looking down at her designer clothes and prissy hair, he hated her for her arrogance. He was hers for forty-eight hours. He'd received the papers often enough to know what she was buying wasn't reconciliation or burying the hatchet—unless it was in his back. But he'd be damned if he'd make it easy for her. He intended to make it as difficult as possible. Just like she'd made it for him.

His eyes captured hers across the room. No one here could afford to outbid that kind of money and they both knew it. For a moment he was annoyed that she would show off that she could. Her eyes glinted with triumph and he smiled thinly, knowing for now she thought she'd won. But she didn't know who she was dealing with. He wasn't a callow youth down on his luck any longer.

In the next moment, her tongue snuck out and wet her lips, and he knew this was a once in a lifetime chance. Because if he was hers for forty-eight hours, she was also his. She'd get what she paid for and more. And he'd get his pound of flesh. All for the bargain price of two grand towards Betty's chemo.

"Going once...going twice...sold to the highest bidder, Ella Turner, for two thousand dollars."

Dev bent and retrieved his shirt from the floor and hopped down off the stage. He squeezed Kate's arm on the way by, a kind of thanks-for-trying gesture. He forced what he hoped was a good-natured laugh at the catcalls from those that knew very well he had a history a mile long with Ella.

And then he walked out of the bar.

Chapter Two

Ella scrambled to write her check and hurry outside, her heels clicking furiously on the scratched wood floor. The article had slipped to a corner of her mind. She knew Ruby Shoes and its patrons well enough to fudge that part of the article. She ignored the calls from old neighbors and long-ago acquaintances. What she really wanted to know was where Dev had gone. And how on earth she could convince him to sign the papers so she could leave this backwoods town behind her forever. He *owed* her now. She had just made sure of it by buying him off the stage. He was at her beck and call for forty-eight hours. What she wanted would take a few seconds.

The air outside had cooled and it kissed her skin, damp from the close atmosphere inside the bar. Her feet halted abruptly. Dev was leaning against the tailgate of his pickup truck, the same two-tone brown Lariat he'd driven to the courthouse on their wedding day. It had several more dents and rust spots now. He'd put his shirt back on. Thank God. Because seeing all those planes and angles while he'd flashed that knowing dimple at her had been torture. It had brought back memories she'd rather stayed buried.

She didn't want to be married to him any more. That had nothing to do with the fact that seeing him strip off his shirt had made her want to touch him. Taste him. Make love to him.

It was plumb crazy, but her libido had spoken loud and clear—it was listening to her memory, not her head.

A small grin curled up the side of his mouth and her breasts tightened. She needed him to sign the decree. Now. So she'd never have to see him and his sexy grin again. So she could finally move on.

"What are you doing here, Ella?"

His voice was a little soft, a little rough, and it rode the endings of her nerves, sending shivers up her spine. She straightened her shoulders. There was no way on God's green earth she would let him know he got to her in any way. And he sure didn't want to spend two days with her. Not once in twelve years had he made any effort to see her whatsoever. She'd let him off the hook all for the price of his name beside the X.

She lifted her chin, tucked her notebook more firmly into her handbag. "Does it matter?"

He nodded, slowly. "You bet your designer bag it does. And I'm pretty sure paying two thousand dollars for two days with me wasn't the reason. Though we could have a lot of fun in two days, don't you think? For old times' sake?"

Memories of bygone days swirled around her, seducing. "Shut up, Dev," she murmured.

He boosted himself away from the truck and came closer. She could smell his woodsy aftershave, feel his body invade her personal space and hated herself for liking it. Craving it.

He leaned into her ear while the hairs on her neck stood up from the close contact of his breath on her skin.

"You could have had me for free."

She planted her hands on his shoulders and pushed, skittering away on her heels. "I...I was sent on a story. It had nothing to do with you, you egomaniac."

He snorted, looking at the ground and scuffing it with the toe of a sorry looking boot. "A story. Of course. Makes sense to send a big-city reporter to a dive like Ruby's for some trumped-up charity event."

He wouldn't understand. He never had. This was why she'd sent him divorce papers several times, even back when the legal fees to do so meant she had to eat peanut butter for a few weeks. "There's something bigger at work than Betty Tucker's illness, you know." She straightened her blouse and raised an eyebrow at him. Damn straight. There was corruption from the top down, and Betty Tucker was only one victim. Bringing an exposé against Betty's insurance company would guarantee Ella her choice of assignment.

"I bet Betty Tucker wouldn't think so. Do you think a woman who might be dying cares at all about how many newspapers get sold in Denver?"

Damn him. He'd always had a way of making her feel small when that wasn't what she'd meant at all. Couldn't he see it was a greater-good issue? But Dev had never been one to see the big picture. He'd had the most annoying tunnel vision of anyone she ever met. Right and wrong. Black and white.

"I don't expect you to understand," she huffed, lifting her nose and moving to walk past him to her car. Forty-eight hours. Hmph. If he'd sign by the X right now, he'd be off the hook and she'd consider it two thousand dollars well spent. They could end this farce of a marriage and get on to their respective lives.

He reached out and grabbed her arm.

"You never expected me to understand, Ell." The words were laced with unexpected venom. "I understand a hell of a lot more than you think."

His fingers burned holes in her sleeve and she fought back the thrill of excitement thrumming through her just by having his hands on her again. It shouldn't happen after all this time, but he'd always had that effect on her. She pasted on the brightest smile she could muster. "Brilliant. So why don't you tell me what I'm thinking right now?"

He still had a firm grip on her biceps and she tilted her chin way up to look at him. Even with her heels on, he was taller than her. Over six feet of manly sexiness. Her gaze caught on his lips. Those lips had known every inch of her when they'd been little more than kids. She blinked. Back then he'd been the solution, not the problem. The savior, not the devil.

"You're thinking, how am I going to get Dev to sign those papers I've got sitting in my car?"

She twisted out of his grip and stomped to the car as his knowing laughter echoed behind her. She *had* been thinking exactly that. Along with wondering how his mouth would feel over hers when she wanted nothing more than to be free of him. For good. How was it possible to think both at the same time?

"Well. You're smarter than you look," she answered, determined he not know the effect he was having on her. If ever she'd needed confirmation that she'd done the right thing by not looking back, here it was staring her in the face. She couldn't even manage a simple conversation with him without losing perspective.

"Yep. So where to now, Ell? Because according to your terms of purchase, we've got forty-eight whole hours."

A shiver went through her at the possibilities. But possibilities got a girl absolutely nowhere. "You sign these now, and we'll call it even. Both of us free as a bird."

He came towards her, walking with that lazy long stride she remembered. His T-shirt was untucked and had a line of dust across it from the floor inside. She wanted to reach up and brush it off. But she didn't. She couldn't touch him. Not after the way her body had reacted when he'd whispered in her ear.

She backed up against the door of her car, her breath hardly moving her chest.

"I'm in no rush, Ella McQuade."

"You never were." She said it with a snarky twist so he'd be sure to get the insult. "And don't call me that."

His body was warm as they hovered only inches apart. If she leaned forward the slightest bit they'd be touching in several places. Her body strained against her clothing while her head warned her to stay put.

"Why not? It's your name."

"Not anymore."

He lifted his hand and traced a finger down her sleeve. She shivered. He'd always been that way. He'd always known what a simple touch could do to her. They'd learned together, discovering all the special spots. Only now it was worse. Now they were older, wiser. Knowing he still had that effect on her hurt. She should have moved on by now. Moving on was the entire reason she'd brought those papers to begin with.

"It is until I sign those."

"Please, just sign them then. Sign them and I'll be out of your hair for good."

His finger went up her sleeve and down again. "Not yet. Come back to the house. I still have some things of yours anyway. You can pick them up."

"Devin." She looked up at him, censoring him with her eyes. "You know that's not a good idea."

Dammit, saying it did nothing more than give credence to the attraction shimmering between them.

"When have you and I ever had good ideas?"

The door to Ruby's opened and shut again and she sighed.

Did she really want to argue this in a public place?

"Almost never," she admitted.

"Forty-eight hours. That's my deal, Ell. You spend the weekend with me, and at the end of it I'll sign your precious papers. You'll be free as a bird, as you said."

He would have to make this more difficult. He was on the verge of giving her the very thing she wanted. Only he would make her spend two days with him to get it. The last place on earth she wanted to go was the house where they'd lived for a whole month before she disappeared. But she was an adult. She could control her urges, couldn't she? How was she going to handle tough assignments if she couldn't handle one itty bitty little husband?

"Maybe I'd like to be rid of you as much as you'd like to be rid of me," he continued, the softness of his voice belying the returning barb.

"If you'd wanted out, all you had to do was ask. Or sign the papers any of the times I couriered them to you."

He regarded her strangely. "I had my reasons." He put his hands in his pockets. "So what will it be, Ell? Those are my terms. How much do you want the divorce?"

She slid out around him and heaved a sigh. "You take your truck," she conceded, her stomach curling with dread. This had disaster written all over it, but she had to see it through. "I'll follow you."

The house looked exactly the same as it had the day she'd left it behind, and she knew without a doubt it was a huge mistake to be here. She'd never intended to see it again. She wasn't sure what bothered her more: the memories it contained or what it represented now. A love that had blossomed within its walls or the life since spent in neutral. It certainly brought home the fact that she and Devin had wanted different things. She had moved on to the city and a career. He was still here, driving the same truck, living in the same…well, shack, for lack of a better term. They didn't belong together. That much was clear.

As she negotiated her car through the ruts, she had a moment of remembering. God, they'd been kids. Barely over eighteen and taking over a small home next to his parent's south meadow. At the time it was what they'd wanted, rather than living in the house down the road with Dev's mother and father. They'd wanted privacy. They'd wanted a place to spend what little time they had together alone. But his parents had moved on now, gone from even the main farmhouse up the road. She shouldn't be surprised Dev was still here, she supposed. His casual approach to life was one of the things that had driven her crazy. His casual satisfaction with the status quo rather than burning ambition.

She pulled up behind his truck, watched him get out and slam the door. The fact that he was content to live this way was a big part of why she left in the first place. She'd been scared of being stuck for the rest of her life in a dead-end town with a dead-end job.

She'd had dreams. They both had. She'd wanted more than a cabin and babies, a mundane job and cards on a Saturday night. She'd never wanted to struggle to make ends meet the way her mother had. And she'd wanted to see things, do things. She'd gotten a taste of those things the moment she'd driven through the university gates and it made her realize that Dev would have kept her here until babies came along, making it impossible for her to do anything else.

She'd been so naïve. Thank God she'd realized it when she had, before their marriage had gone on for too long. She'd found the world to be a lot bigger and more exciting than Backwards Gulch. And she'd never looked back. Not once.

"You gettin' out or sittin' in that thing all day?"

She sighed, reached over and grabbed the envelope with the papers before getting out of the car. She wasn't sure what he was playing at, but she'd go along. For now. Her first priority had to be getting this part of her life in order. If that meant putting up with Devin for two measly days, she'd do it. She wasn't an unsure girl any longer. She was a grown woman with a mind of her own, used to getting her own way.

"A gentleman would have opened the door."

Dev stared at her from the front porch, his weight on one hip. "Yeah, he probably would have."

"But you're no gentleman."

"You said it."

"Why are you making this so hard for me?"

For a second she thought he was going to respond and her insides curled, suddenly afraid of how he'd answer. Was it revenge for what she'd done? Hate? Or maybe he simply hadn't cared at all. She looked around at the cabin. Maybe he didn't care...about anything. Their eyes clashed...his blue sparks that lit a fire in her she hadn't felt in a very long time. She watched as his gaze trailed down her blouse, her skirt, to her toes and back up again, assessing. Oh, he cared about something. She got that message loud and clear. And if the jumping in her stomach had anything to do with it, she knew *exactly* what he cared about. Forty-eight hours stretched interminably in front of her.

Oh, no. She wouldn't go down this road again. She'd been a sucker for his baby blues as long as she could remember. She squared her shoulders and met his gaze boldly. Challenging.

He shrugged, turned around and slammed the screen door behind him.

A sound of exasperation bubbled out of her throat as she stamped her foot. The man was so frustrating. She gripped the papers tighter in her fist and went after him. Maybe if he'd cared the least bit he'd have come after her when she'd said she was leaving. But no, it had always been this nonchalance. If he didn't give a damn he could just sign the decree and be free of her once and for all. She hadn't missed the look he'd given Kate McGrew tonight. What the hell was between them anyway?

And for a long moment she stood with her hand on the door handle, wondering how many women he'd been with since she'd walked out on their marriage. She was fully aware that she had no right to ask. But the thought of him with another woman was like acid to her insides. It shouldn't be. She'd given up her rights to him years ago, practically if not legally.

"Ell, you want a beer?"

She inhaled sharply and stepped inside.

It was sparse but neat, and exactly the same as it had been when he'd carried her over the threshold. Cupboards to the right, fridge on the left, situated between what would have been termed the living room and kitchen area. Her heart gave a little lurch as she remembered that day. Why now, after years of putting them aside, did the memories seem idyllic, uncomplicated? Those times had been anything but. Yet inside, a tiny corner of her remembered how it felt to belong to him, to have that bit of hope and feeling like he would make everything all right as they began their lives together. That night, on their wedding night, he'd made love to her for the first time.

She heard the sound of him popping the top off a bottle of beer, the creak of couch springs as he sat, his back resting on a homemade afghan crocheted for their wedding by his grandmother. She pulled herself out of the memory. That wasn't what was real. She'd realized it soon enough. What was real was her job and her life back in Denver. Her nostrils flared as she heard the old springs twang as he shifted his weight, reaching for a remote control. She was so beyond this.

He turned on the television—it was the bottom of the ninth of the game that had been on at Ruby's. She stared at his profile and didn't miss the miniscule quirk to his mouth. He was playing with her, she was sure. Acting like there was nothing more important at stake than one out and runners on first and third. Trying to get on her nerves. Two could play at that game.

She ran her finger along a scarred end table, rubbing her thumb against the dust there. Maybe a small part of her had hoped he'd done something more with his life. That he wouldn't be stuck in the same pattern like everyone else in this backwoods town. But maybe that was asking too much.

"Take a load off, honey."

"No, thank you."

"Suit yourself."

"You could sign the papers and be rid of me."

He didn't answer, just leaned back into the cushions of the sofa. After several long moments she started to feel like an idiot, standing in the near silence while he tipped back his beer and pretended to watch the game. Finally she went to the battered stuffed chair and sat on the arm rest. Tears stung the backs of her eyes. This wasn't how it was supposed to be. She had been right, and everything she'd seen and heard this evening seemed to bear witness to that. So why couldn't she hate him? She needed to hate him. And somehow she couldn't. Somehow, just being with him for this short amount of time made her feel like she'd never been away. She remembered the first time he'd kissed her, right here on this porch. She remembered the fire that always seemed to erupt between them. The first time he'd said he loved her, his voice hadn't quite decided what pitch it wanted to be. The last time, on the morning she'd driven away, his voice had been deep and sure and gritty with sleep. She didn't want to remember. It hurt way too much.

The game finished and he half-turned, sitting sideways on the couch and looking up at her. He took a long drink of Coors, licked his lips. She stared at the path his tongue made.

"Ell."

"Don't," she whispered, hating the indulgent tone. She made a point of staring, unseeing, at the television that was now playing commercials. The picture blurred through the sheen of moisture in her eyes. She hated herself for that little bit of weakness. She would *not* cry.

"Ell," he said, stronger.

She tore her eyes away and looked down at him, feeling like utter and absolute hell. This was supposed to be easy. She didn't love him anymore. She'd moved on, built her own life. So why was it so painful simply seeing him, hearing his voice say her name?

Because up until October—almost exactly twelve years ago—hearing her name on his lips had been all she'd ever wanted. Because since they were kids, even before puberty, they had always been there for each other. As their voices and bodies changed, so had their awareness. But it hadn't changed the other closeness, the friendship. And hearing him say "Ell," in just that way, just now, brought it all flooding back. She'd never had to feel completely alone because Devin was there. It made her want him again, almost desperately, and she hated that he could accomplish all of that just by saying her name.

His brows relaxed slightly and he attempted a smile, as if

he could sense the path of her thoughts. "Silver Bullet cures all ills." He held up his bottle.

"Not tonight, Dev." It came out all husky and thick and she cleared her throat. Tonight, she realized, they were finally saying goodbye to their marriage. It suddenly took on an importance far bigger than she'd anticipated.

"Come on, a divorce is what you want, right? This marriage has been over for a long time. Maybe we should celebrate with a few cold ones."

Celebrate was exactly what she'd intended to do—back in Denver. She and Amy were planning to hit the clubs and dance until they closed down—rejoicing in what was to be Ella's newfound freedom and fresh start. But the *idea* of Dev was somehow a very different thing from being faced with his devilish eyes and sexy body. It reminded her of things. Things she needed to forget. She wanted a marriage based on love, independence, respect. Common ambition, if it came down to it. Saying goodbye shouldn't be hard. But it was, and she didn't quite know how to deal with it.

Maybe they could forge a truce over a couple of drinks, have a little honesty about their marriage—or lack of it— without all the pretense. She ran her tongue over her bottom lip. If they did that, maybe she wouldn't have to wait the whole weekend for him to sign. She knew he was doing it to be difficult, and on one hand she knew she deserved it. She'd been the one to walk away, after all. On the other hand, she just wanted to find the quickest, least painful way of getting it over with. She met his eyes, a deep, honest blue that took her breath away.

"Tonight I think you'd better break out the bourbon," she whispered, hoping the fortification would see her through.

Wordlessly, he rose, went to a cupboard and pulled out a

bottle of Jim Beam. He sat it on the table and took two shot glasses from another cupboard beside the sink. Finally, he got a beer from the fridge, flipped off the top and put it beside her shot glass.

"Shots with a chaser," he said, and sat. "Just like old times."

She watched him as he unscrewed the cap and poured two shots of amber liquid.

Then he lifted his eyes to hers...captured her with his gaze as surely as if he'd bound her to the chair.

"To August twenty-second." He lifted his glass. Waited.

He was toasting their wedding date, looking as sober as a man could possibly look when facing his wife of twelve years—especially since he hadn't seen her in eleven years and as many months. In a split second images raced through her brain of that day, of her cheap dress and the courthouse and a handful of witnesses. And with the images, the sensations, feelings. No, no, no. She had to stop this right now. This wasn't supposed to be memory lane.

Her hand trembled as she picked up the glass, but she couldn't speak. She saluted, and tossed the liquor back.

"Whuaaaa!" She gasped as it burned a path straight to her belly. She grabbed the beer and took a long swig, trying to douse the flames licking their way down her throat.

"Atta girl."

He poured another, nodded at her. "Your turn."

"My turn?"

"I made the first toast..."

What could she possibly say? He'd toasted their anniversary, for God's sake. She knew it had been a deliberate jab. She knew this was the time for her to rebut. A couple of shots she could handle. A couple of shots would take the quiver out of her hands and alleviate the nerves jumping around in her stomach. She'd keep her head and accomplish her goal that much faster. She thought for a moment, then smiled sweetly. "To September thirteenth."

His brow wrinkled in the middle. "That's today."

"Yup. And it's the day we undo August twenty-second."

She held up her glass, daring him. Would he drink to it? Their marriage had been over for years. "Well?"

"I haven't signed anything yet."

She paused for a moment. Was that a veiled threat that he wouldn't? She ignored the sly smile flirting with his lips. No, this wasn't the time to back off. This time she'd one-up him and get her way.

"Come on, McQuade. Swallow your pride and the shot. At this point it's just a formality, and you know it."

His hand was steady. "You know how much I stand on formality."

She very coolly cocked one eyebrow at him. Challenging back.

He swore, but he drank.

The fire of the alcohol sent a languid warmth through her and she smiled. A few drinks and a signature, and they could both move on with their lives. They already had been. Well, mostly. She'd made a good life for herself, in a profession she loved. Good friends. A nice apartment. But she hadn't been completely happy in Denver. And she knew a lot of it had to do with tying up loose ends. She looked at Dev, with his tousled hair and almost invisible freckles under his deep tan. Yep. Definitely a loose end. Always keeping her tied to a past she was desperate to forget. Looking over her shoulder.

He poured a third shot as she lowered the Coors to the table. She watched as he lifted the glass, turned it in his fingers, staring at the dark liquid like it held a secret. A smile curled along the edges of his mouth and she bit down on her lip. She stared at his fingers, his long, very capable fingers, and her pulse skipped a beat. Maybe the shots weren't such a good idea because she was starting to think less about the objective and more about Devin. She crossed her legs under the table. He would not get to her. He wouldn't.

"To your virginity."

Oh, sweet mother. Her cheeks flamed red instantly, the heat scorching, curling around her ears. She coughed and lifted her glass as he said the last words…

"And to mine."

She gulped down the bourbon and slammed the shot glass down on the table. "You're not playing fair, McQuade."

"You wanted me to play fair?" His eyes widened with feigned innocence. "What's the fun in that?"

"When did you turn so sentimental? Anniversaries and first times? Come on." She snorted to hide how much his toast had touched her heart and chased the shot with a quick gulp of cold beer. She still held a certain amount of misplaced pride that she'd also been his first. They'd learned together. Had wanted to learn together and she'd been so afraid of getting pregnant he'd done the honorable thing and married her first. It was her stupid, fairy-tale mistake that she'd said yes. They should have just bought a pack of condoms and gotten it out of their system. If they had they wouldn't be here right now.

"And you've really been around to see whether I was sentimental or not, I suppose." His words hit the mark and he sat back in his chair, glared at her.

"I get that you're angry that I left."

"Angry?" Truth was coming out as the bourbon was going in. His voice had raised and he took a breath and let it out again. He picked up his beer bottle. "Angry didn't quite cover how I felt. Or how I feel about you, Ella McQuade."

"Don't call me that!"

Her shout echoed through the tiny house.

"Your turn," he said quietly.

Ella had always been able to handle her liquor, but three shots in twice as many minutes, on the back of the awful wine she'd had at the bar, made the edges suddenly blur. It was as if someone had warmed the air, making it fuzzy, and yet it had an angry edge, like something in the shadows waiting to strike. She concentrated on pouring from the bottle as he watched her closely. She'd just ignore the fact that he was hovering. Or that he'd just said that he felt something for her after all.

She slowly pulled his shot glass over. "I don't know why you're fighting me on this, Dev. We both know it was over long ago. It doesn't make sense to hang on any longer."

"Maybe I need you to understand some things first."

She put the bottle down carefully, deliberately. Slid his glass back across the table. "Things like what?"

His grin was fast and devastating. "If I told you, it would be me telling you rather than you understanding."

She forgot about the toast and merely tossed back the shot, needing to regain the upper hand. "Go away for a decade or so and I come back to find you're a woman, getting all philosophical. When did you become all in touch with your feelings, Dev? You've been reading those self-help magazines, haven't you? Or maybe watching too much Oprah in your spare time?"

He matched her shot. His arm seemed to move slower than before as she watched him drink and lick his lips. She needed to slow down. Someone had to stop pouring.

"Tell yourself what you want, Ella. You're two thirds of the way drunk and the rest of the way deluded."

The edges blurred further. She should have eaten earlier instead of driving straight through. Or she should have stuck with having a beer rather than suggesting bourbon. *Idiot.* Either way, he was right. At least about the first two thirds. And he was apparently as sober as a judge. Bastard.

"Yeah, well screw you and your bodyweight, buddy."

He chuckled, a warm, fuzzy sound that tingled from her toes clear up to the top of her head. A bit louder until he was laughing. The sound was catching. She couldn't help it. She joined in. It was all so surreal. She'd vowed she'd never come back to this house again. And yet here she was. Getting three sheets to the wind with her *husband*. The world had gone crazy.

"What the hell are we doing here, Dev?" she asked on a long sigh.

"Getting drunk."

"You mean getting divorced."

"I like my D word better."

She leaned back in her chair as the room tilted slightly. A button on her blouse popped and she looked down, surprised, but she didn't move to fix it. She looked over at Devin, leaned back in his chair, his legs extended on either side of the seat. His T-shirt was rumpled and she was treated to a recall of him pulling it off while on stage tonight. The way his muscles had looked, all firm and rigid and strong. How the hollow of his hips had just been hinted at by his low-slung jeans. Her body tingled all over because she knew. She knew what was beneath the jeans, the shirt, all of it.

It was the last thing that should be on her mind.

Chapter Three

Devin looked over at her and knew instantly what direction her thoughts had taken. It would be a mistake. Getting her slightly drunk had been a way of looking for an advantage, to maybe get her to finally admit what she'd done. To let down her guard the slightest bit. He'd wanted her to admit she was *wrong*. He'd made that ridiculous forty-eight-hour bargain because he wanted to punish her. He wanted to play with her feelings the way she'd played with his—without caring. But he couldn't be that callous—it wasn't in him—and now he was getting more—and less—than he'd expected. Oh yes, he knew when he was beaten, and this was it. Now there was a bit of a peep show going on at his kitchen table, and he was still sober enough to know what he was feeling was pure lust. The kind he'd never really felt for any woman but Ella.

Her bra was white, cut to a deep plunge, and molded her breasts perfectly. A shadow clung to the cleft below her collarbone and he wondered what it would taste like. If it would taste the same as he remembered. A little salty, a little sweet and one hundred percent Ella.

Her hair was falling out of its tidy sweep and he was reminded once again of how she'd turned her back on them to pursue what, this? Fancy clothes and a chick car, living in the city? That was her life now. And maybe he'd goaded her tonight.

No maybe about it, he had. He was still angry deep down. She had walked in here, willing to believe this was all there was. She thought his life was this cabin and a second-hand sofa and a bottle of bourbon. She honestly didn't know anything about him. Hadn't taken the time to find out, when she could have so easily. He wasn't sure if that was funny or just sad.

And yet, he'd seen her face when he'd toasted their wedding day. He desperately wanted to believe the kind, trusting Ella he'd married was still in there somewhere. That despite all the changes both of them had seen, at their core, where it counted, they were still the same people. And for that reason he knew he couldn't give in and touch her. Not yet.

"Do up your buttons and go to bed. I'll sleep on the couch."

Her saccharine smile wobbled on the edges as she stood, a bit unsteady. She balanced herself with her hands on the table before kicking off her heels. "What, chickening out, McQuade? There's still half the bottle left."

"Being sensible."

"Tsk tsk. But I'm the sensible one, remember?"

It was a real job not to get up from his chair and take her in his arms. He remembered exactly how sweet and soft she could be. But he couldn't. He was the one who had to remain in control. He wasn't helpless anymore—this had to be on his terms. It had been many years since he'd let anyone call the shots in his life, and he sure wasn't going to let Ella—beautiful or not—do it again.

"Not at this moment, you're not."

She wobbled and he stood quickly, reaching out and gripping her arm to steady her. "Jeez. You didn't have *that* much."

She turned brown eyes on him, sorrowful and long lashed. They were like a punch straight to his gut. "I don't drink bourbon anymore."

He closed his eyes. Lord, what was he going to do with her? He'd seen her across the bar and he'd damn well wanted to teach her a lesson. He'd been waiting a long time for her to finally get the courage to show up, to end their union with a little respect. He was the one holding the cards. So why was he finding it so difficult?

"Besides," she continued. "I paid two thouzzand dollars for fordy-eight hours of Devin McQuade. Scooter Brown said so."

He caught the slur. "You just did it to get me to sign the divorce papers." It helped slightly to remember she'd come with her own agenda.

"Well, I've got you now. What *shall* I do with you? You're at my beck and call, remember." She ran a fingernail down his arm, making a shiver race down his spine.

Beck and call indeed. His blood surged at the innuendo. Why now? She hadn't sent papers for a few years. Was it something...someone back in Denver making her come all this way? A boyfriend? The thought did nothing to cool his heels. It only served to resurrect some buried territorial instinct where she was concerned.

After the last time he'd sent the courier away, he'd thought she'd given up. That had been nearly two years ago, so what had changed? Why else would she be here, if not to free herself up for some other guy? He clenched his teeth. A husband was a heck of a skeleton in the closet, wasn't it? He wondered if the new guy had any idea Devin even existed.

Or maybe she'd heard about his change in circumstances and wanted to profit from it. They'd never signed a pre-nup. At eighteen and poor as church mice, there'd been no need.

She was a reporter. It wouldn't have been that hard, he realized. For a moment he dismissed the notion. The old Ella wouldn't have considered it. But he wasn't sure he knew this new person hanging off his arm. Perhaps all this guff about the cabin and him never moving forward was just a cover. Perhaps she knew all about him and what he'd done with his life, and she was after half of everything. In this age of technology, it was difficult to believe she didn't know about DMQ. All it would have taken was one Google search to figure it all out.

He tried to turn her and steer her to the bedroom. Good Lord, she was going to have a head on her in the morning. He hadn't meant for her to get this tipsy. Of course, she was a little bit of a thing. Compact, a bundle of energy and passion. Her breast grazed his hand and he gritted his teeth. If she hated him now, she'd really despise him in the morning if they slept together. Almost as much as he'd hate himself. He was in control. It was time she knew that. If she thought she'd get what she came for easily, she had another thing coming.

He'd take what he wanted first.

"Dev?"

"Yeah?"

"You're so tall. You know that, right?"

He smiled. She could make it so hard to hate her, especially when she used that soft, slightly plaintive tone like she had to have it or she'd just *die*. "Yeah, rumor has it."

"No, I mean really tall. Tall like women like their men to be tall. So that we have to tip our head back and look *way* up." She sighed, her sex-kitten eyelids drifting half-shut. "Sexy tall."

"Shut up, Ell." A muscle ticked in his jaw and in another strategic location. If she kept looking at him that way he was going to find it very difficult to put her in bed and walk away. But he'd be damned if he'd give in to her tonight. No matter what it cost him.

They took two steps.

"Dev?"

He sighed.

"Yes, Ell?"

She gripped his other arm so she was facing him, looking up at him with her dark eyes and lips red and slightly puffy, ripe to be kissed. He swallowed, hard. God, how he'd loved her.

She did it then, standing up on her tiptoes, melding her mouth to his, the flavor of the bourbon seducing them tongue-to-tongue. His mouth opened in an instinctive reaction to feeling hers on it. He lifted one hand and cupped her head, sending the prim twist askew, hairpins dropping to the floor. Her breasts were firm against his chest and she let go briefly to tug at the hem of his T-shirt.

"Take this off," she murmured, pulling the hem up over his abs. "Not in front of the bar. Not for Katie McGrew." She said the other woman's name with just enough venom for Dev to enjoy the surprising fact she was jealous. "Take it off for *me*."

For her. The words fired him up and he reached behind his head, grabbing at the collar and pulling it over in one swift movement. This much. He'd allow this much. He'd let her get a good hard reminder of what she'd thrown away. But no more. They didn't dare go any further.

Her fingers trailed down over his skin, the sensitive skin of his ribs, down his shoulder and to his elbow. "Mmm."

He slid his hand over her blouse, allowing himself one gratifying handful as he kissed her fully. Despite the Jim Beam or the years that had passed, her taste was as familiar to him as the smell of sweetgrass. Ella. His Ella. He kept his mouth fused to hers as he blindly undid the buttons of her blouse, filling his hands with her breasts once the fabric fell away. Her hand slid around to cup his bottom through his jeans.

A murmur sounded deep in her throat and he knew he had

to stop, reminded himself that sex right now would only make things worse. He couldn't afford to spend Saturday dealing with post-coital fallout. She'd blame him for...what? There would be something, he was sure, and it would be all his fault and none of hers. No, tonight he'd leave her wanting more. He was the one with the self-control here. He'd get her to damn near ache for him, the way he'd ached for her for months after she'd abandoned him. And then maybe he'd sign her precious papers. After his lawyer'd looked at them. His terms, he reminded himself. She owed him that.

It took all his resolve, but he backed away, leaving her standing stunned and utterly beautiful.

"Go to bed, Ella." He pushed her towards the single bedroom. "If you don't, you'll hate yourself in the morning far worse than you hate me right now."

She turned and stared up at him with dazed, hurt eyes. He couldn't bear for her to argue, so he walked out into the cool September air, letting the screen door slap behind him.

Banging. Someone was hammering something, and each sound wave was a shock to her brain.

Oh God.

Ella rolled to her back and closed her eyes. She was in Dev's bed, the sheet twisted sideways and the comforter up to her chin. As her legs twisted in the cotton, she realized she was in her underwear. How had that happened? Had she undressed herself or...or had Devin had to help? Why couldn't she remember?

Groaning, she pressed a hand to her forehead and rolled over, away from the light. Her blouse and skirt were in a crumpled clump on the floor beside the bed. Slowly bits and pieces of last night filtered back into her throbbing brain. Arguing. Then doing the shots. And then...

She sat straight up in the bed and groaned as all the blood rushed forward and suddenly down. She clasped her hands to her aching head. She'd kissed him. More than once. And she'd had her fingers on his skin. And he'd had his fingers on hers.

But they hadn't slept together, of that she was sure. She sighed heavily, relief sluicing through her. That would have been a big mistake. But she also remembered it was Dev who had sent her to bed like a naughty child and she wasn't sure the humiliation of that wasn't just as bad. At least she'd had the wherewithal to undress herself. That much she remembered as her brain began functioning again.

"Drink this."

His voice, deep with a bit of gravel in it, came from the doorway. He leaned against the jamb with a shoulder, holding out a mug with steam coming off it.

"Coffee?" The aroma wafted across the room. Now *that* she could live with.

"Yeah." He pushed himself away from the door just as she realized the blankets were down around her hips and she was sitting there, still in the bra she'd worn last night. She went to grab the covers, but his sideways grin made her hands stop. There was no sense playing modest now. No sense playing shy. She was supposed to be a modern woman, after all. And the bra was far more modest than the bikini she'd worn in St. Lucia last year.

Dev had seen all of her lots of times. But it didn't stop the odd feeling of shyness at being in his bed in nothing but her skivvies.

"You need something for your head? You're not looking so good." His hand reached out and touched her mop of hair and she cringed. "Is it bad?" He sounded genuinely concerned. The jerk.

She wanted to reach out and throttle him, but that would take physical effort, and sitting here scowling was far more preferable to collapsing in a post-drunken heap. "Yeah, it's bad. So thanks for the coffee."

"I brought your bag in from your car. I thought you might like to brush your teeth."

"Thank you, Dev." This politeness and courtesy was almost as nerve-wracking as being at each other's throats. It certainly threw her more off balance. She only had to stay until tomorrow and he'd give her what she wanted. Clearly, sweet talking over a few drinks was not the correct approach. A blush crept hotly up her cheeks as she remembered how horribly she'd failed at that strategy. Instead she'd practically thrown herself at him. She was no better than one of those floozies at the bar last night who'd whistled and catcalled when he'd taken his shirt off.

Today she'd have to try something different, and try to keep this happy little reunion short. Above all, there couldn't be a repeat of last night's behavior. Maybe today straight shooting was the way to go.

"I appreciate the coffee, but you don't have to be nice to me."

"Is there some reason I shouldn't be?"

There was an edge to his voice she hadn't ever heard before. She could easily list a dozen reasons and proceeded to name the top contenders. "Because I left you within two months of our marriage and I'm here for a divorce?"

His expression soured. "There is that. But then...I am at your beck and call for another thirty-six hours."

"I didn't realize butler service was part of the deal."

"Just thought I'd keep you in the style you're accustomed to," he jabbed, heading for the door. "Oh, and breakfast is almost ready."

The thought of food made her stomach lurch and she stopped the mug on the way to her lips. "Breakfast?"

He laughed in response to her weak question. "You'll only feel worse with nothing on your stomach, Ell. The liquor will stew in there for hours. Trust me." He looked back over his shoulder but the smile was gone. "I learned the hard way."

She got the feeling he was talking about more than a few nights out with the boys, and stared at the empty doorway. What did he mean he'd learned the hard way? They'd snuck down to the river with a contraband bottle now and then as teenagers, but he'd never been a drunk. She wondered if her leaving had left more of an impression than she thought. He'd never come after her, and she'd assumed he was ambivalent about the whole thing. But clearly not. Had he attempted to drown his sorrows?

It didn't matter. What mattered was somehow convincing him to sign the papers today. Then she'd be on her way back to Denver, she could finish up her article and life would get on once more. There was a position opening up on the East Coast in the next few months and she knew someone at the paper. If she could break this story, she might have a good chance of getting it. There was a big world out there waiting, and being married to Dev—even on paper—had meant that she never really felt free to explore it. Looking over her shoulder.

Gingerly, she stepped out of the bed. She considered pulling on her skirt, but it seemed pointless. The bathroom was just across the hall. She looked out the door, but all she could see was Dev's back at the stove.

Her bag was sitting beside the toilet. She grabbed her

change of clothes—a pair of jeans and a snug pullover—and her makeup kit. Within five minutes she'd showered, and in another five she'd brushed her teeth, put her damp hair up in a ponytail and brushed on a little bit of makeup. The outside felt better than the inside, but she could smell breakfast in the kitchen. Not that she'd admit it to him, but it smelled *good*. All she'd eaten last night was a packet of peanuts she'd picked up at her last fill-up. It was no wonder the bourbon had gone straight to her head.

She was standing in the doorway to the short hall when he spoke, his back still to her. "Sit down, it's ready." She didn't know how he knew she was standing there, and she uncomfortably moved ahead and sat at the small table. A faint smell of spilled liquor surrounded it and her stomach lurched. Last night she'd definitely been stupid. But being faced with him after all this time...and realizing quite unexpectedly that not all of her feelings had faded...

All in all, bourbon had been the easy way out. She'd only tried to justify it with machinations of getting her own way.

He placed a plate in front of her—scrambled eggs and a couple of slices of buttered toast. Suddenly she felt a craving for something sweet.

"Jam?"

"Out."

"Marmalade?"

He laughed. "Marmalade? Are you serious? When have I ever eaten marmalade?"

She picked up her fork, recognizing that he probably didn't have a stocked kitchen, and feeling the need to point it out. How in the world did he live? But she didn't want to fight anymore, and he had at least made an effort. She'd just have to do without an adornment for her toast. "Thanks for breakfast,

Dev." She speared a piece of egg and tentatively placed it in her mouth. It tasted good, and she knew it would sit just fine. She nibbled on a corner of her toast. He took the chair opposite and scooped up eggs, layering them on his toast, and took a huge bite.

"If you'll sign the papers I can be out of your way after breakfast."

He put down his toast and took a drink of coffee. "That wasn't my deal. You got somewhere you need to be? It's the weekend. You can't work *all* the time. Maybe you should relax. De-stress."

She didn't have anywhere she had to be, exactly. At least not today. But it seemed better to get this over with as quickly as possible. Like ripping off a Band-Aid.

"I don't know why you insist on me staying the weekend. It's not going to change anything."

He calmly ate more eggs.

"You're not going to tell me why?"

"I have my reasons. Maybe if you tell me why you need to leave, I'll think about it."

"Denver. I have to finish up my story and get it to my editor first thing Monday morning."

"Ah," he nodded, knowing. "Of course. Work." She stared at him blandly. "Sorry. *Career.*"

She could have thrown her egg at him the way he used that patronizing tone with her. And the fact that he was sitting there as unperturbed as could be, a layer of sexy stubble on his chin and his perfect teeth glaring at her every time he smiled. She wished he could understand what her job meant to her.

"It's what I do. You know that. And this article is part of a bigger picture, and if I do a good job I can move up at the paper."

"And that's what you want? To move up?"

"Of course it is. I don't want to be in the Lifestyles section forever. I didn't spend all that time and money in school to cover tea parties and write articles on the season's recipes. I want to hit the big time. I can't do that where I am. I need to go after the big stories. And after that..." She let the idea hang. It wasn't the right time to tell him about the opening in Boston. And it wasn't important. After this weekend, nothing she did would be any of his business.

His fork hit his plate and his eyes darkened. What had she said to set him off now?

"So what, an article about how the insurance company's giving Betty the shaft? She's just another victim in a long list, right? Might as well make an example of her. What the hell. Bonus if it furthers your career at the same time."

She didn't understand why he was so angry about it. This was the way life worked. "So what if it is? I hate to tell you, but people make news. The healthcare system is a farce. Betty's case is one of many. Why shouldn't I work on a story that might change all that? The media has a lot of influence, you know. It's *important.*"

He pushed out his chair, taking his half-empty plate with him. It clattered on the counter top. "Cut the noble cause bit. You're not interested in change. Reporters have sniffed around before. Betty isn't a face for reform, Ell. She's a human being. A human being who's really sick. And you're trying to profit from it. You and the rest of the vultures."

Ella put down her toast and dusted her fingers off on her jeans. "So is it me you have the problem with or my profession in general?"

He dumped the remainder of his breakfast in the garbage.

"Maybe both. The old Ella would have cared about more than paper distribution and a promotion."

She swallowed. She did care, but why did it have to be one or the other?

It was impossible to be here and not be assaulted by memories in every corner. Young, idealistic, full of dreams that in hindsight seemed so simple, so naïve now. He was going to start his own contracting business. She was going to get her degree and write the great American novel. They'd been so full of themselves, so oblivious to the way the world really worked.

"The two don't have to be mutually exclusive, you know. I do care. I just grew up."

He spun around from the sink. "Grew up? You went away to college and never came back. You didn't just spend time and money to get where you are. You also turned your back on our marriage. You sold out."

The bitterness soaking his words cut into her. "No, I didn't." She pushed out her chair and stood too. "I just stopped being a besotted teenager and started living in the real world." She looked around the sparse house. Had he changed anything since she left? Anything at all? "You might try it some time."

He laughed then. "Right. You go off to the city and suddenly your world's the real world and everyone else's is what, the Stone Age?"

"They don't call it Backwards Gulch for nothing." She fired the words back at him. "Look at this place. The furniture's the same. Your truck's the same. You probably get up the same time every Sunday morning and go fishing. Am I right?"

"And there's something wrong with that?" His eyes narrowed, criticizing.

"God, yes!" Couldn't he see that he was going nowhere staying in this hell hole? Didn't he ever want more? "I can't believe I was considering finishing the article here. I mean, my laptop's all well and good, but I'd have to have Internet, wouldn't I? And God knows *that's* not going to happen."

"You're right. There's no Internet here. And I'm perfectly okay with that."

"Of course you are."

"There is technology outside of Denver."

She sniffed. "Yeah, right. It sure as hell isn't here. Don't you ever want more than horses and fishing? What about your dreams? Don't you have any of those?"

Devin clenched his fingers. He'd known this argument was coming, but he'd be damned if he'd slap her in the face with the truth. Of course he had dreams. And he had wanted more. Most of it he'd achieved and he was damn proud of DMQ. If this cabin was anything, it was an escape from the world he'd learned about very quickly after she'd gone. He liked it this way. Quiet. Simple. Disconnected from the rat race.

But he'd waited a long time for her to make her way back and she needed to figure it out for herself. If she didn't...it would truly be over. He wasn't going to beg. But he wasn't going to let her off easy either. She knew nothing about the man she'd left behind. Knew nothing of what he'd been through since she walked away, or what he'd accomplished. Or how difficult it had been.

"You've focused so much on your own ambition that you don't see anyone else. All you see is what you want to see. You did sell out. I know because I remember your dreams as well as mine."

She laughed, a bitter, harsh sound that made him want to punish her with another kiss just to wipe the sarcastic grin off her face.

"You mean your dreams of owning your own business,

Dev? How you were going to make us rich one day? And look at you. You're still right here. Exactly where I left you."

"Don't turn this on me right now." He fought to keep his voice level, the words of his own redemption sitting on his tongue. No. Either she didn't know the truth or she was goading him, and he didn't like either option. If she was completely oblivious to his success she'd have to work for the truth. By the end of this weekend he'd show her exactly what she'd walked away from. What she could have had and had so blithely thrown away.

"Do you even remember what you wanted back then? What happened to those dreams? What happened to you wanting to be a writer—and don't tell me you are one because you know that's not what I mean. You weren't thinking of journalism when you said it. You wanted to be a novelist. You had plans. *We* had plans." He let the words hit their mark before he continued, quieter but no less biting. "Now look at you. Do you care about anything at all?"

"That's not fair! How dare you judge my life? You know nothing about it!" She stepped forward, crossed her arms across her chest as her dark eyes snapped with fury. "You stayed here like I knew you would. Never changing. Never seeing!"

He gritted his teeth. He saw very well, thank you. He had seen a damn sight more than she knew about. Fury bubbled up as he remembered going through the dark years, wanting her beside him but unable to ask. "Talk about blind! You see what you want to see. So maybe I'm not signing the papers today. Maybe I'm doing *you* a favor."

"Me a favor."

He heard the ripe skepticism and it made him angrier. She knew nothing about him anymore. And that had been *her* choice. The girl he'd known—loved—would have made an effort to understand. He'd missed her, the girl he'd said he'd spend the rest of his life loving. Cherishing. He had missed her every single day since she'd left him. For a long time he'd pretended he hadn't, but he was older now. He was too old for self-delusion. But maybe he was deluding himself right now. Maybe that caring, loving girl was gone forever. Maybe she was so caught up in herself, in her quest for glory, that she'd truly left him behind like yesterday's trash.

He was no one's trash.

"I grew up too," he muttered.

"You what?" And her derisive laugh echoed through the house.

It made him almost mad enough to sign the papers right then and there, but he knew he'd regret it. There was more. More he needed to know. He had to protect himself legally. If he'd learned any lesson it was that all agreements needed to be in writing. And if she was pretending, and she did know about DMQ, he needed to guard his assets.

There was also more she needed to see—bits that went beyond dollar signs. But right now he could only see his own frustration ripping away any sense of perspective.

"You know what, Ell? You're really pissing me off right now." He went over to the fridge, took out a canned juice and snapped the top open viciously.

"Then let's just end this farce of a marriage right now," she asserted.

"You'd like that." He nodded. "You'd like to take your snooty hair and pointy little chin and drive back to Denver pleased with yourself that you were right all along." Maybe it was time for him to tell her exactly what he thought. Maybe it was time to clear the air and let the chips fall where they may.

"Here's the thing, Ella McQuade. And don't tell me it's Turner because you were sure as hell proud enough on the day we were married to tell everyone that you were a McQuade now. Do you suppose your leaving was easy for me? Huh? What do you suppose happened? I just read your letter and said, 'Well, that's it' and went on my merry way? I didn't. It wasn't easy for me. I'd wanted you since I was old enough to know what sex was and I loved you before that. So why in hell would I make it easy for you now? Huh?"

His fingers trembled around the can as Ella stared at him, clearly shocked into silence.

"I've got stock to check on." He turned away, pulled on a pair of boots at the door and picked up his half-empty can.

"What am I supposed to do?"

He stopped and looked back. There it was. Just a flash, but for the smallest moment she looked unsure, vulnerable, like she had last night when he'd tried to put her to bed and she'd kissed him. There was something. He couldn't have been wrong about her for all those years. What would it take to bring the real Ella back? Or was she too far gone?

"I think an independent, capable woman like yourself will find something. Oh, and I left you something on the coffee table. You can do with it what you like."

He banged out of the door and stalked down the lane to the barns.

He went inside to begin the morning routine, slamming through the mindless task of feeding stock and turning them out into the crisp fall morning.

Ella knew nothing about his life. And he'd be damned if he'd tell her.

Ella grabbed a paper napkin from the table, balled it up and threw it at the door.

He was singularly the most obstinate, exasperating man on the planet.

He knew nothing about what it had taken for her to put herself through college, the student loans or the jobs she'd had to take to make ends meet in the beginning. She'd worked hard. And she had a good job. She had great friends. She had accomplished that. On her own.

She went to the fridge looking for something that might resemble fruit or yogurt. There was butter and milk, a few condiments and a package of sliced meat. That was it. She sighed, closed the door and rested her forehead on it. Why couldn't this be easy? Why did he have to fight her every step of the way? She closed her eyes, remembering the feeling of his hands on her breasts last night and how close she'd come to asking him to share the bed. They had all this *garbage* between them and yet one touch had almost rendered it all irrelevant.

But being with him would have set up another long list of regrets. Wanting him sure didn't change who she was or who he was. Or who she wanted to be when it was all over.

She wandered to the living room area and stared at the coffee table.

On it was an old electric typewriter, the cord folded neatly with a rubber band holding it together. She went over and ran her fingers along the cold gray frame. Thought of the black keys with white letters, how the indentations in each key felt under the fingers. She sat before it and rested her fingers on home row. Different than any computer keyboard. He'd kept it all this time. It was a side of Devin very different from the side that had yelled at her this morning.

She ran her nail along the space bar, sighing. He'd bought

it out of his savings when they were in twelfth grade and had given it to her for Christmas so she could start her first novel. When she'd gone to college, she'd said she'd come back to get it at Thanksgiving. She remembered the morning she drove away from him, her new husband, and how she'd cried all the way up the interstate. They'd agreed on school. And they'd promised that once it was over, they'd really start the life they'd promised in front of the judge at the courthouse. She was going to be a writer. He was going to work for his dad until he could start up his own contracting company. He'd taken part of each paycheck and played the market—she remembered him saying he'd always been good at math and how proud he'd been when he'd made his first money in the market when other boys in school had been playing football and hanging out at the corner store.

The backs of her eyes stung as she realized she'd been the one to throw their perfect life away. She'd been the one who'd broken promises. She'd gone away but she hadn't come back like they'd agreed. And this morning had shown her how much he hated her for that.

She wiped beneath her eyes. Today she'd run a few errands. And tonight she'd make him see why finalizing the divorce was the best thing for everyone.

Chapter Four

The simple house was built nearly square, set on an average street that was slipping towards shabby. The grass in the surrounding front yards was brown, and the flower pots sitting on the steps of a handful of houses were brittle and dried. Ella pulled into the gravel drive, noticed that the paint was cracked and peeling around the windows but the front porch was a new, blinding white. Compared to several of the properties nearby, Betty Tucker's was surprisingly well-kept.

Especially for a woman who had recently had a mastectomy and was looking down the barrel of chemotherapy.

When Ella knocked on the door, she didn't know what to expect. That made her nervous, always had. She'd grown up only a few streets away, in a house even smaller than this one. Two tiny bedrooms, a cramped kitchen, living room and a bathroom where the shower always dripped, no matter how many times her mother had tried to fix it. As she stood on Betty Tucker's doorstep, the old claustrophobic feelings came back, smothering. The hours she spent home with the door locked, too young to be left alone but there because there was no money for daycare. The times she'd wanted to get out but her mother had needed to work.

Occasionally, her mother had brought home boyfriends. Most of them had been nice men. A few had ignored Ella and considered her in the way. For the most part though, during those times, life had been good. They'd done more things, like swimming in the river in the summer or the odd trip to the movies, and her mother had laughed more. Until the relationship died a slow death and Ella was left to her own devices again.

Then there was the night she'd waited, and waited. The night her mother never came home after falling asleep at the wheel following a double shift at the truck stop out on the highway.

The door opened, and Betty pushed the screen door outward while Ella stepped back, shaken out of the harsh memories. "Ella Turner. Well, this is a surprise."

Ella tried to smile up at Betty, her lips quivering slightly as she worked to dispel the memories. That was the past. It wasn't who she was anymore. She was here to do a job, that's all.

"Good morning, Betty. I'm surprised you remember me."

"Of course I do. Devin used to talk about you all the time."

Ella felt her body flush as she remembered his hands on her skin less than twelve hours before. "Devin and I go way back. I hope I'm not bothering you."

"Come on in. Heard you were at the bar last night. Figured you'd want to talk."

Ella stepped inside but let the screen door slap behind her as surprise temporarily made her forget to close it properly. "You did?"

"Everyone in the Gulch knows you work for that paper in Denver now."

They do?

Betty gestured towards a chair and went to the sofa, sitting down heavily. "Lordy, I seem to tire so easily these days. Sit down, please."

She perched on the edge of the chair, noticing the living room needed updating but that it was devoid of even a speck of dust. "I don't mean to intrude..."

Betty flapped a hand. "What gets me is I don't understand why some paper in Denver is interested in little old me."

Ella let out a breath and smiled. "That's easy. It's because you're being treated unfairly."

"So's a lot of folks."

"Yes, but you're..." She almost said *one of us*, and paused. One of us? But Ella wasn't part of the *us* anymore. Hadn't been for a long, long time. "You're somewhat local. And the community support you've received has gotten attention. It's my job to take that and use it to get the attention of lots of people—including law makers and even the insurance company. But only if you're comfortable talking."

"I don't have anything to hide."

"May I tape this conversation then? Just to make it easier to remember? Then I won't have to pause to take notes." Ella reached inside her bag and withdrew a tiny recorder.

"I don't know..." Betty paused, her gray eyes suddenly unsure. The relaxed, comfortable woman that had answered the door had disappeared, and now Ella saw what she'd expected. A woman who was afraid. Not necessarily of the tape recorder, though it seemed to be the item that caused the shift. But afraid of the changes life was dealing her. Ella felt a shaft of sympathy. Betty was going through this all alone and with the added worry of money.

"Don't worry. I promise I won't use what you say against you in any way. You're the victim here. I want to help. This just helps me keep things clear."

"I don't want to give the insurance people any more ammunition, that's all."

Ella tried to smile reassuringly. "They can't use the truth against you, and I promise I won't twist what you say. You have my word."

"I guess it's all right then."

Ella clicked the record button and put the recorder on the small coffee table so Betty could see it running. She felt a wistful sentimentality knowing Betty trusted her so easily even though they were relative strangers. And yet Devin, who had known her since they were children, didn't trust her at all.

"Why don't you take me through what's happened since you were diagnosed, Betty. That's a good place to start."

Betty stared at the recorder and rubbed her lips together. Ella smiled, understanding the older woman simply needed to be put at ease. "I grew up two streets away. I remember you working at the drugstore in Durango." Ella pushed aside the memory of slipping in to buy Tylenol and Band-Aids for her mother's blisters. "Are you still there?"

Betty swallowed. "Yes, I'm still there. Not so much lately though."

"I expect you had to take some time off to recover from the surgery."

"Yes, I did." Betty's shoulders relaxed and she sat back on the sofa, looking into Ella's face rather than at the recorder. "Only as much as I had to. I have to keep working. Bills to pay."

"Bills like ordinary house bills?"

"Yeah, them too. And medical bills."

Ella crossed her legs and relaxed. "Because your insurance won't cover your treatment?"

The ice broken, Betty related her struggle. Her very basic

insurance didn't cover cancer treatments, and since she was already diagnosed they wouldn't take on extra coverage either. "I've got a lawyer working on it, but he said it could be weeks tied up in red tape. Or longer. And each week that passes, the odds work more and more against me."

A lawyer? Ella wrinkled her brow. That was a surprise. "If you don't mind me asking, how is it you have managed to afford a lawyer when things are so tight?"

Betty smiled then, a ray of sun through the stress of illness. It wiped the tiredness from her eyes and Ella realized that Betty wasn't as old as she'd thought. She couldn't have been past fifty. She was a woman who had a lot of life left to live. If the cancer didn't get her first.

"Mark Randall offered to do it for free."

Mark Randall—the name didn't ring a bell for Ella. And he was taking on her case pro bono? "Is Mr. Randall a friend of yours?"

"Oh no, he's a friend of Devin's, you see. That boy...he's been a godsend. I couldn't have managed this far without him."

Ella tried to swallow her surprise. Devin? She looked around the very plain, dated room. The furniture was at least two decades old; the paint needed freshening, but everything was as neat as a pin. Betty worked at the drugstore, Devin was still up in his ramshackle cabin in the woods. And yet he knew a lawyer named Mark Randall? One capable of a high profile case?

"Devin? What's he done?"

Betty tucked her legs beneath her on the sofa now, finally relaxed while every nerve ending in Ella's body seemed to be tightening. Devin was involved in this? But why? How? He wasn't doing such a great job of managing his own life, after all.

Then she remembered him walking out on stage last night,

all faded jeans and sexy boots and dimples. Damn him. Back less than twenty-four hours and already she was feeling sucked in to the Gulch and all the things she'd wanted to get away from in the first place.

"Oh, that Devin. He put the bug in Ruby's ear, you know. To hold that benefit last night. I was planning on going, but I ended up at the Medical Center." She gestured weakly at the right side of her chest. "Still healing. I got a bit of infection, but they put me on antibiotics right away."

"I'm sorry."

Betty waved a hand. "That's the least of my worries, so don't trouble your pretty head about it. Heard the night was quite fun at the end." She aimed a sly grin at Ella. "Heard you up and bought Devin for two thousand dollars too. I guess I should thank you for that."

Ella covered her fluster by reaching forward and shutting off the recorder. "Lots of boys on the auction block last night, not just Devin." She tried to make her voice light, not sure if she succeeded or not. "Some I haven't seen since high school."

Betty's eyes held a film of moisture. "Don't I know it. The people around here..." She broke off, swallowed as emotion thickened her voice. "Well, I don't know what I did to deserve it, but they've been a blessing. And none more than your Devin."

Devin again. Ella was starting to get annoyed with how often Betty was singing his praises, and ignored the deliberate addition of "your" to his name. He wasn't her Devin. Not anymore. Nor would he be again. So what if he'd been right about Betty. Their marriage was over and before the weekend was out he'd sign the divorce papers and they'd wash their hands of each other.

"I'm glad he's been helpful," she offered weakly, putting the recorder in her bag. She'd gotten what she came for. It was time to leave.

"Helpful?" Betty pinned her to the chair by the exclamation and the happy smile. "He came by and mowed my grass a few weeks ago before everything turned brown, and put a new coat of paint on the porch. And he showed up the day after I was home from the hospital, arms full of groceries. He stocked up my kitchen and made me eat. Then he went and hired Eunice Sharpe to come and clean each week until I'm back on my feet. He's a good man. Like a son to me."

Ella's heart sank. Could Devin do no wrong? Betty's glowing testimonial did as much to make Ella feel like an outsider as anything had since she'd returned. Saint Devin. Meanwhile Ella knew how she must look to the people of Backwards Gulch. She was the one who'd run away. She looked like the girl who thought she was too good for them. It was so far from the truth.

Oh no. She'd spent the last decade of her life trying to prove herself. To be worthy. To be *something* better than where she came from—the orphan of a deadbeat father and an overworked mother.

But that was a little closer than she wished to look. "Thank you for taking the time to talk to me this morning." She smiled, sliding her bag over her shoulder and straightening her sweater as she got up from her chair. Betty rose too, a little slower but with a warm smile.

"You're welcome. It was right nice seeing you again too, Ella. You grew up so pretty, and you made something of yourself. Good for you."

Ella's eyes stung. The praise was unexpected and felt almost...motherly. In Ella's world, that was absent, and it was bittersweet.

On impulse, she went forward and gently hugged the older

woman. "Take care of yourself. And good luck, Betty."

Betty carefully hugged back, then gave a light cough and backed away. "You get on now. I hear the winning bids last night got forty-eight hours of beck and call service. You get back to your Devin."

Ella blushed and headed towards the door.

"Ella?"

At Betty's soft call, she turned back, touched once again by the soft, sad look in the woman's eyes.

"Did you want to add something more?" She could have her notebook out in a flash. Sometimes these little incidentals were the gold mine of quotes. The little throwaways that could be the true heart of the story.

"Just...I know your mom would be proud of you. That woman worked herself to the bone. I'd hate to see you do the same thing and miss out on something great."

Was Devin the something great she meant? How could he be? Their relationship had ended years ago. And Betty...there was so much that she didn't know about what had happened. It was far more likely the woman was waxing nostalgic because her mortality was staring her in the face.

"Take care," she repeated softly, and shut the door behind her.

Ella stopped at a supermarket in Durango and picked up enough groceries to get by for a few days—the prospect of the packaged ham and white bread in Devin's kitchen wasn't the most appetizing. She wasn't sure what he ate but it couldn't be much from home—not after seeing the contents of his fridge. It was clear he was going to hold her to the whole forty-eight hours, and they needed to eat. She refused to let it be scrambled eggs and take-out.

As she wheeled the cart through the store, she mulled over her conversation with Betty. What would it have been like if she'd stayed in Backwards Gulch? She picked up a package of salad greens and sighed. Even the sound of it was ludicrous. It was impossible to picture herself stuck in Dev's cabin, day in and day out. Why would she, when she could have her downtown apartment and her friends, a job with a byline and an actual social life? Restaurants and events and real shopping rather than a turn around the corner market. Plays and concerts instead of fly fishing and baseball games on television.

And yet she couldn't get past the fact that he still got to her, perhaps even more so now that she knew how great he'd been to Betty. What had he gotten out of it? She wished she knew.

As a reporter, she longed to ask him.

As a long lost wife seeking a divorce, she couldn't afford the distraction.

He'd been her first love. Her only love, if it came to that. She'd never been comfortable doing more than going on a few harmless dates back in Denver, simply for appearances' sake. She was married, and that meant something to her even if it was in name only. And lately she'd started thinking it was going to be a long road if she wouldn't have a relationship because of a piece of paper. She was stuck. And Dev had to set her free. He was a detail that would be sure to come back and bite her in the butt later. Maybe if she were free legally she'd be able to get him out of her mind too. Maybe Amy was right. Maybe she needed it legal so she could have closure.

She wheeled the shopping cart to the checkout, grabbing a bottle of wine on the way through—no more hard liquor for her. If she were going to convince Dev to let her go, she couldn't pick another fight. She'd cook him a nice dinner. After all, her mother had taught her early on that you caught more flies with honey than vinegar, and this morning's argument had left a definite acidic taste in her mouth. They'd sit and talk like adults. Surely they could manage that much.

And tomorrow she'd take her notes and her laptop and drive back to Denver. She'd write her story, lambasting the insurance industry for failing the ordinary American. God willing, she'd get her promotion. She and Amy would go out on the town to celebrate. She could leave Backwards Gulch—and her past—behind, right where it belonged.

She drove her Miata through Durango, thinking about all she'd heard and seen today. Maybe Devin really thought she was exploiting the situation for her own agenda. He'd certainly accused her of it. And maybe she had been, in part. But not today, not after seeing Betty. She wanted to help. And if it meant Devin got on her case about a story, so be it. Writing was what she knew how to do. It was the only way she could think to bring notice to Betty's plight, to possibly help others like her.

As she headed towards Devin's, she realized that the focus had to be on the woman herself, not the numbers. The quiet strength, the appreciation of her neighbors and friends. The woman was anything but bitter, even though she had reason to be. Ella had been touched by it. That was what she wanted to write about.

When she got back to the cabin it was eerily silent. It seemed to echo with scenes past and she fought to ignore them, unloading the bags and putting everything in the fridge. It was only after she'd put the roast in the oven that she heard a rhythmic thunking sound coming from the backyard.

She put on her shoes and followed the sound.

Devin was chopping wood. A stack of logs lay to one side,

the pieces landing in a pile as he split them with sure, strong strokes of the axe. She watched, heart skipping a beat, as he lined up a log, hitting it once, twice, three times, splitting it in half. He took the halves, treating them to the same barbaric swings before tossing all four pieces in the growing pile. She looked at him in a different light. She knew the cabin was as run-down as it had ever been, yet he'd helped Betty with groceries and household chores. Had he gone without to do it?

He put his axe down alongside the stump he used as a platform for the wood. Ella opened her mouth to call out, but shut it again as he stripped off his shirt and the T-shirt he wore underneath. Sweat glimmered on his brow, his chest, creating a sheen as he lifted the axe again.

Ella stared with blatant fascination. His shoulders and arms bunched as he lifted the axe over his head, his chest broad as he brought it down, and every single muscle in his upper body froze for a millisecond as the axe bit and held in the wood until he pulled it out again. The muscles above his gloves corded as he gripped the ash handle. Her blood heated. She'd known that seeing him again would be difficult. But she hadn't quite known how difficult. Or that she'd be tempted. To stay forever? Hardly. But his sculpted body was enough to make her twitchy. To touch him...taste him...yes, definitely.

"Enjoying the show?"

For a moment she wasn't sure he'd spoken, as his arms kept swinging the axe. He stopped and threw the pieces on the pile, then stood back, his weight on one hip, leering at her.

She had no idea how to respond. She'd been caught out. Any smart comment she might have made ran clear out of her brain. And to admit her thoughts would be a big mistake. Like touching a match to gasoline.

"Go stuff yourself."

He laughed. "That's the best you can do? The old Ella wouldn't have self-edited."

"The new Ella has a little more class, in case you didn't notice."

The moment the retort was out of her mouth, she felt stupid. What was it about him that made her so defensive? Now she sounded uptight and snobby.

He merely raised an eyebrow, making her feel even more foolish. He took the axe and brought it down in one more stroke, leaving it impaled in the stump. He reached down and got his clothing but didn't put it on. "I need a shower." He walked past and she smelled him...good clean sweat, wood shavings and hay. It shouldn't have made for a good combination, but it did. It was a manly scent. Capable and like the outdoors. His chest gleamed and she wondered if it would taste salty against her tongue.

He stopped in front of her. "Well? Did you have a good afternoon?"

I will not argue. I will not pick a fight, she told herself. Honey, not vinegar. At the same time she rolled her fingers into her palms to keep from touching him.

"I did, thank you. And I brought some food back."

"You didn't need to do that." He frowned.

She smiled, determined to keep things friendly. "Least I could do after you fed me this morning. Mother Hubbard's cupboard couldn't be barer."

He shrugged. "Suit yourself." He started to walk away towards the house.

"Dev, I..." She paused, suddenly unsure. She wanted two very different things here. She wanted to be with him. Her body ached to know if his touch would be the same. And yet she wanted him to let her go.

"What?"

He half-turned and her gaze was caught again, looking at the hard wall of his chest. "I bought pancakes for breakfast. Then I have to leave to go back to Denver. I have a lot of work to do."

She didn't say it, but she knew he'd registered her implication—the papers had to be signed before she went.

His eyes were cold, his lips a firm line. "Suit yourself," he repeated, harder this time.

Ella followed him inside. "Dev, don't do that." The door shut behind her. "I told myself all afternoon I didn't want to fight with you."

"So you thought you'd butter me up with a home-cooked meal, I'd sign the divorce papers and off you'd go to your bright and shiny life."

It stung when he put it that way. "I prefer to call it an olive branch."

"Maybe I'm not interested in an olive branch with you. Have you thought of that?" He threw the shirt on a chair and pulled the T-shirt over his head, covering up his magnificent chest. His eyes glinted like icy shards.

"What do you want from me, Devin?" Her voice raised, frustration getting the better of her. "I can't change what happened. I can't roll the clock back twelve years."

"Would you want to?"

Silence fell. It was heavy with questions and dark answers. Would she? She didn't think so. She'd built a good life for herself. She'd proven she was smart enough, capable enough to stand on her own two feet. But seeing Dev again reminded her of what it had cost her. She'd given him her heart once. And

71

she'd never quite gotten it back.

"I don't know what you want me to say. I just want you to sign the papers."

He came forward, put his hand on her cheek. She closed her eyes against the touch, suddenly gentle in a hostile world.

"Will saying goodbye to our marriage be that easy for you?" His words were hardly more than a whisper.

No, she realized, and hurt sliced through her. But she couldn't tell him that. Not in a million years. Telling him would only make it worse.

"I said goodbye to our marriage a long time ago, Devin."

He stepped back.

"I'm going to have a shower."

He walked away and she let him. Even as much as she wanted to shove a pen in his hand and tell him to just get on with it, she knew the only way this was going to work was to let him see it was over. Truly over. That the distance between them was too great.

The shower turned on and she thought of him standing beneath the spray, naked. A yearning pulsed through her. She wanted to strip off her clothes and join him as the hot water pounded their skin. To slide the soap over his hard muscles. To feel the touch of her body against his, slick with water. Her breasts tightened as she thought about his hands on them, his mouth...

Damn, staying here was starting to get to her. There were too many reminders. Thank God she'd be going back tomorrow.

Chapter Five

Devin took his time getting dressed, sitting on the bed in his clean jeans wondering what the hell he was going to do about her. She could swear up and down she wanted a divorce, but he'd seen her face earlier. It had been with perverse pleasure that he'd stripped to the waist while splitting wood. She'd wanted to touch him just as much as he'd wanted to touch her. Hell, he'd taken to chopping wood he didn't need just to try to get her out of his system, to stop remembering how it had felt to hold her last night. To taste her, if only her lips. To want her as much—maybe more—than he'd wanted her years before when she'd belonged to him.

Only his distraction technique had backfired when she showed up, looking seventeen again in a pair of faded jeans and a soft pink sweater.

When Devin came out of the bedroom Ella had tiny potatoes bubbling on the stove and the makings of a salad going into the single bowl he had in his cupboard. He paused, simply looking at her for a moment. So damn beautiful. She still looked like the winsome girl he'd taken to prom, when she'd been freer with her smile. It was like age had forgotten her. Her skin was flawless, a perfect cameo setting for her dark, expressive eyes and pretty lips. She looked up from the vegetables and her hands fell still.

He wanted her so badly it almost hurt. It was a damnable thing, wanting a woman you couldn't have, especially when that woman happened to be your wife. Even worse when that woman was determined not to be your wife any longer. He couldn't tell her the truth. He'd never know how she really felt—or what had truly happened that autumn—if he told her his side. It would color everything, and she'd feel sorry for him. He'd rather die than have that happen.

He'd thought he wanted get some answers before he let her go. But she was fighting him every step of the way. He wouldn't give in easily. The last time he hadn't been able to fight for her. But now he could. He could at the very least find out why she'd ended their marriage with a letter. And then—if their marriage were finally going to be over—it'd damn well go out with the farewell they hadn't ever had.

"I hope roast beef is okay."

He cleared his throat, trying to push away the image that had blossomed in his brain at his decision. She looked small and...innocent standing there tossing a salad. His brow furrowed. Yes, tonight they'd be together one last time. But only if she felt the same way. His body tightened at the thought. The only way he ever wanted her was willing, warm and pliant with desire.

He tried to remember what she'd just said—oh yes, the roast. "It's fine."

She nodded, looking back down at her salad. "I did some background work for my article this afternoon. I ran some errands and ended up at Betty's. You...you might have been right there. I'm still writing the story," she said, and he noticed how her cheeks flushed. "It's my job. But I don't want you to think I set out to make a spectacle of her. I know she's a nice woman. It might be my job but it doesn't mean I can't help too."

"Fair enough."

"Really?" Her head lifted, and he saw the surprise in her eyes. He knew he'd been heavy handed with her this morning. And it had been more about himself than Betty. Once more he fought off the guilt at not telling her everything. And he called *her* selfish. But Ella didn't know about his personal issues with the healthcare system. She didn't know how all the money he'd saved for them to get their start had gone to hospital bills.

Perhaps the more important truth was that she hadn't cared enough to find out, had she? Perhaps he should remember *that* each time he was tempted to take her in his arms, or when he felt himself softening towards her. She'd left and never looked back. The only time she'd made contact was when she sent the divorce papers.

Still, her voice held a trace of contrition and he almost believed her when she said she wanted to help.

"Really, Ella. I might think a lot of things, but I don't think you'd deliberately exploit Betty Tucker for your own gains. At least not completely."

"Thank you. I think." She smiled and put the salad on the table. "I did want to ask you though...she mentioned you've been helping out a lot. Why is that?"

Her voice was smooth, the very pointed question ensconced in velvet. And the answer was one of those truths he wasn't willing to share with her yet.

"Is it wrong to give a neighbor a hand? I haven't done much."

"You helped organize the benefit, took her groceries and put her on to a lawyer. That's what I'd call much."

"I knew Mark from before. He..." Devin paused, needing to be partially truthful even as he covered up more of the story. "He handled some of the farm stuff with Mom and Dad."

Farm stuff. More like them selling off the farm for the cash Devin had needed. Paying them back had been first on his agenda.

"Still, it's what you'd expect a family member to do, you know?"

He reached over and picked a cucumber out of the salad while his heart beat a hundred times a minute. "Betty doesn't have any kids to help." He forced a smile. "When did you say we were going to eat?"

She looked away and he exhaled, hoping that was the end of the interrogation.

"It's almost ready. I bought some merlot...but maybe you'd rather have beer."

He almost laughed, part out of relief, part disbelief. She really *didn't* have any idea, did she? There was no way Ella was that good of an actress. She truly thought this was his life. Just this. She saw him as Devin McQuade, lowbrow redneck. For a flashing moment he considered telling her about all the changes in his life, about DMQ and his condo and the new development on the west side of Durango. But then...no. If she decided to stay it had to be for the right reasons. Not because he'd suddenly become someone different on the outside.

"Wine's fine. I don't think we need a repeat of last night, do you?"

"No," she murmured.

But Devin couldn't stop thinking about it. Much still stood between them, but he couldn't erase the memory of how she'd felt in his arms again. How her lips had teased and beguiled, how her fingernails had trailed down his flesh. They weren't kids anymore. They'd grown up a lot since eighteen. Foolish as he knew it was, he wanted to claim his wife. He wanted to believe in her again. But if she came to him now, it wasn't going to be because she'd had too much to drink. He wanted her clear-headed and saying his name in the darkness. He wanted it so that he was the only thing she saw, felt, tasted. He wanted all of that first, before showing her how his world had changed.

She finished putting the meal on the table, while the newfound amicability pushed against its constraints. He didn't want to be polite. He didn't want to dance around facts anymore. He watched her hands as they poured wine into a glass and handed it to him.

Her eyes twinkled at him as she lifted her glass. "I think toasting is probably a bad idea at this point."

"Oh, I don't know." He took one step closer so that he could almost feel her body against his. "How about, for old times' sake?"

Her smile faltered. "For old times' sake?"

"There you go." He grinned and tapped the rim of her glass with his. Drank deeply, letting the flavor envelop his tongue. The taste reminded him of her. Soft, full, seductive, yet in an un-ostentatious sort of way. Her hand trembled a little as she lifted her goblet. Good. A tiny drop of the ruby-red liquid stained the top of her lip. Before she could take a breath, he moved in, dipped his head and drew it away from her mouth with his tongue.

She stepped back like she was on fire. "What are you doing?"

"You had some on your lip."

"Then give me a napkin!"

He laughed then and saw her lips thin as she got angry Lord, he loved her angry. Her cheeks flushed and her eyes snapped, ready to take him on. Oh, he hoped so. He really, really did. He was dying to remind her of what she had discarded.

"As you can see, I don't have any."

She pushed him aside, going to her seat instead and sitting. Her eyes flashed with irritation. "I don't know why I tried to do something nice for you," she railed. "I thought we could have a nice civilized dinner."

"It's because you love me." He smiled blithely and took another drink of wine.

She nearly choked on her first bite of potato.

"I'm here for a divorce, remember?"

"Yes. How could I forget when you remind me every two minutes?" Devin sat and picked up his knife and fork. He cut his slice of beef and speared it, examined it, then looked up at her. "But they are two very different things."

"What are?

He swallowed. "Love and our divorce.

"Are you saying you still love me, Dev? Because that's pretty impossible. You told me exactly what you thought of me this morning."

"You were quite right when you said I was angry. I was. I am. I'm not sure I'll ever stop being angry about it, to be honest."

It was work to continue eating, but that was exactly what Devin did.

"But do you still love me?"

Ella put her free hand between her knees and squeezed, suddenly nervous at how he'd answer. She hadn't planned on asking either. But nothing about this trip had gone as planned. She certainly hadn't planned on feeling like she did. She'd been back for a few hours and she'd been immediately sucked into the past. She didn't want him to love her. She didn't. And yet she knew if he said no, she'd be crushed. How irrational was that?

"Let's just say I never stopped loving the girl I married." His voice was low, tainted by what she would have sworn sounded like sadness. "But whether or not you're her, I don't know."

She knew without saying a word that this was what he'd meant this morning. And in some ways he was right. Silence enveloped them and they went through the motions of eating, but her heart wasn't in it. She'd made promises. Maybe she shouldn't have, but she had. And not for the first time, she felt the smallest bit guilty for leaving him the way she had. She'd been a coward. She'd been so afraid.

Dev crossed his knife and fork on his plate and sat back, swirling the wine in his glass. "That was great, Ell. Really good."

"Thank you."

Silence settled around them, awkward and seductive.

"Why did you really come here?" His gaze pinned her from across the table, and she looked down at her lap.

"Because you never signed the ones I sent you."

"So you really came here for a divorce."

"Yes."

"After all this time."

She lifted her head, squared her shoulders. "Asked and answered."

Silence fell for a few moments.

"Why didn't you sign them?"

Her whispered words echoed through the kitchen. Dev looked away for a few minutes. When he looked back, her heart nearly broke from the tortured expression twisting his face. She knew she was to blame for it, no matter how he answered, and she felt guilt spiral through her, knowing she'd caused him so much pain. That she'd been capable of it. No one had ever loved her like that. Hated her like that.

"You wrote me a letter, Ell. I got a piece of paper in the mail that said you thought we'd made a mistake and you weren't coming back. You'd realized you wanted more and that we should have known better. That we were just kids. But I wasn't a kid. I loved you like a man. And I hated you with a man's hate for a long time because you were a coward." He ran a hand through his hair, closing his eyes. "Every time you sent papers through your lawyers, it made me more and more angry. I wouldn't sign them because I wanted you to have the courage to come and end it to my face."

Tears quivered on her lower lashes and she refused to blink, knowing it would send them down her cheeks, and she didn't want to cry in front of him. She was ashamed. Hearing him echo her earlier thoughts only made the cut deeper.

"I'm here now. You've got what you wanted." Her voice was rough, her throat clogged. "So why haven't you signed them? Are you just trying to punish me?"

"Maybe." He lifted an eyebrow. "Maybe I am. Maybe I'm just angry enough that I demanded you live through forty-eight more hours of my company before you go away. Maybe I needed to see for myself how hard you've become, thinking that would make it easier to finally let you go. The city changed you. Maybe some of the Ella I knew is still in there. I don't know." His gaze delved into hers, and she was gutted to see pain there hiding in the blue depths. "I waited twelve years for you to come. For you to have the guts to do what you didn't the first time. To look me in the eyes and say goodbye rather than using a piece of paper and a postage stamp."

She didn't blink, but the tears rolled over her lids anyway. It did feel so very final. And more painful than she'd anticipated. And at last the question she'd always had surfaced.

"Why didn't *you* come after *me*?"

He looked away, swallowed heavily. "I kept hoping you'd come back, realizing you'd made a mistake."

She shook her head, sniffled. "You mean you were too proud."

Something dark glittered behind his eyes, something she hadn't seen ever before. Dev was hiding something. She couldn't say why or how she knew. Maybe it was reporter's instinct. But he was definitely holding back. Was he afraid of showing her his feelings? Was that it? Would his pride not let him reveal how she'd broken his heart?

"Maybe I was," he agreed, but it didn't quite ring of the truth.

"And then too much time had passed..." she prompted.

His jaw clenched, a muscle ticking there. "Yes. Time. And now you're going back tomorrow."

"I have to," she acknowledged, and was surprised at the wistful note in her voice. Was it regret? No, she couldn't possibly want to stay longer, to prolong the ending. It was already proving to be harder than she expected to say goodbye.

She had her home and life back in Denver to look forward to. She had theater tickets for Thursday. She was covering the Victorian Ball next month. She had her apartment downtown and lunches with her friends to look forward to. She had to remember all those things, remember what she'd built for herself. The life she truly wanted. In time Dev would see it too.

"Then I guess tonight is it, isn't it."

Was that invitation she heard in his voice?

"It for what?" The question came out on a breath and seemed to hover between them.

Dev scraped back his chair and got up, the sound deafening in the tight quiet around them. He walked over to her chair, took her hand and gently tugged her to standing.

His hands cradled her face, his thumbs rubbed against her cheekbones, wiping away the remnants of moisture from her tears. She was helpless to push him away, prisoner to the tenderness in his touch, so at odds with the anger she'd witnessed only moments before. The gentle gesture made her want to cry all over again, made her want to weep for the memories of how completely they'd loved each other once upon a time.

"The last night I get to do this," he murmured, just before he dipped his head and consumed her with a kiss.

His lips were warm and supple and tasted of the merlot. Ella's eyes drifted closed as she let herself feel his kiss. His hands rested on the tops of her arms, holding her firmly while his tongue plundered her mouth. Sweet, and sad, and oh so final.

She felt a moan rise in her throat and let it escape. The sound echoed through the silent kitchen, adding fuel to the fire.

His lips broke away from hers and he reached behind her head, undoing the clip that anchored her hair, sending it tumbling over her shoulders and down her back. His blue eyes burned into hers, sending jolts of memory straight to her core. *Remember?* they said. *Yes, I remember*, hers answered back. She did remember. How this was only the beginning. How he could consume all of her with the slightest touch. And she wanted him to do it again. One last time.

She worried her lip with her teeth and his grin was lightning fast, sexy, teasing. "You're thinking, Ell."

Her breath came in shallow pants as his laughing mouth touched the side of her neck, suckled on her earlobe. "Don't think. For the love of God, don't think."

"Occupational hazard," she responded, her lashes fluttering. His tongue swirled around her earlobe and that one simple action nearly had her writhing in his hands. My God. The man could patent his tongue as a sex toy. Every nerve ending in her body was standing on edge, and they were both still fully clothed.

"What do you want?" His breath was hot in her ear and she shivered.

What did she want? Him, most certainly. And with his mouth doing naughty things to her neck and his hands sliding over her bottom, she couldn't think any deeper than that. She wanted him. Inside her. Right now. So badly she could almost feel it by memory alone.

"One for old times' sake?" she breathed, dropped her head back while his strong hand supported her neck.

"Oh, I like the sound of that, Ella McQuade," he agreed, his voice devilishly rich.

His tongue teased the hollow of her throat and she couldn't even bring herself to correct him.

He nibbled on her collarbone and her knees wobbled.

"Dev?" It came out as a breathless gasp and she didn't care. "I'm not going to be able to stand much more of this."

Slowly, painfully slowly, he slid his tongue up the column of her neck and along the underside of her lip while she went into complete and utter meltdown.

His mouth left her skin, the trails where it had been suddenly cool in the air. Her tongue darted out and wet her lips. Devin reached down to the table and retrieved her wine glass, handing it to her before reaching for his own.

She drank, the dark seduction of the red wine flavoring her

tongue. He drank from his glass as well, his gaze steady on hers while the world seemed to hum around them.

"Are you trying to get me drunk again, McQuade?"

A slow smile crept up his cheek. "Not a chance, McQuade. I want you fully aware of what we're doing."

Her grin faltered as her stomach did somersaults of anticipation, knowing exactly what was in store. It had been so long since he'd last touched her, but with him only inches from her body it seemed like yesterday. She knew in her head that they had been different people then, but it ceased to matter now. Their hearts were the same. Their chemistry was the same—incendiary. And if she were going to walk away tomorrow, then tonight she was going to give herself one hell of a memory to take with her.

With trembling fingers, she put her glass back on the table and reached for the buttons of his shirt.

One by one she slipped them from their holes until his shirt gaped open, revealing again the chest she'd touched last night, the one she'd wanted to taste this afternoon. She didn't hesitate this time. Her hands slid the shirt out of the way and she touched her lips to the warm, firm skin beneath it, feeling it rise and fall heavily as his breathing grew ragged. She kissed her way down his sternum and then over, running her tongue over a hardened nipple.

"Ell," he murmured roughly.

She ran her fingers down a cotton-clad arm until she got to the wrist and released the button there before moving to the opposite wrist and doing the same. She slid her hands up over his chest and over his shoulders, pushing the shirt off and down his arms. He stood painfully still, frozen in the moment, waiting while she took her time reacquainting herself with his hard, muscled body. She traced her fingertips down the long length of one arm, across the waistband of his jeans, smiling a little as he instinctively sucked in his belly at her touch. Her fingers trailed over to the other arm. Down the middle of his chest, until she finally looked up and saw his eyes were closed, his jaw quivering, and he swallowed thickly.

The little dent in her heart, the one put there when she'd left him, got a little bit bigger. He was holding himself back, letting her take her time. Tears pricked the backs of her lids. He had always been an unselfish lover. She willed the stinging away. It would be so easy to love him again. But loving him and living with him were different. She was smart enough to know that. Too much time had passed for them to pretend they could go back. So she'd love him for this one night. One last time. Tonight she wouldn't be the coward he accused her of being. Tonight she'd give of herself. And when they said goodbye—as they must—it would be without their last memory being one of bitterness.

"Dev."

His eyes opened, startlingly blue in the paling light of the kitchen. Her fingers toyed with the button on his jeans. "Take me to bed, Dev."

He didn't need to be told twice. In a movement that stole her breath, he slid an arm beneath her knees and lifted her into his arms.

Her heart trembled. For a flash of a moment, she was transported back twelve years, to Dev carrying her over the threshold and not stopping until they reached the bedroom. She'd felt the same thrum of excitement, the same throbbing pulse knowing what was ahead. Only now it was different.

She wasn't as innocent. Time had taken that away from her. She knew how life worked. And as Dev took purposeful strides to the bedroom at the end of the hall, she knew this had to be the final goodbye they'd never had. They couldn't turn back the clock. But they could maybe, just maybe, close the book without bitterness. If she could wish for one thing, that would be it. Maybe that was why she'd never come back to end it in person. She'd been so afraid of facing his disappointment, his censure. Having to accept the fact that she'd let down the one person who had loved her best.

Dev laid her gently on top of the covers of the bed. The light coming through the windows was fading, casting half of his face in shadow, accentuating the curves and planes of his muscles. Ella found herself thankful for once for the requirements of manual labor as he braced his strong body over her, his face only inches from hers, his breath warming her cheek, the zipper of his jeans pressed firmly against her core. She let out a breath, shaky with nerves and excitement. Inch by agonizing inch, Dev lowered his body, the muscles in his arms bunching beneath her fingers. His tongue swept into her mouth at the same time as his erection pressed against her. Her hips instinctively rose to meet it, seeking to release the pressure building within her body. Right now it was all centering at the exact point where he was pressed against her.

"Turn on the light," she whispered, her blood singing in her veins with each passing second. If she could only have tonight, she wanted to imprint all of it on her memory, a montage she could play over and over in her mind. Especially how he looked when they made love.

"I want to see you, Dev." She met his gaze in the dimness. "I want to see your face when you're inside me."

He reached over and flicked on a small bedside lamp, casting the room in warm, pinky glow. She made a cradle with her legs and he settled against her, while she fought the feeling that he was back home where he belonged. He wasn't, but the familiarity was enough to shake her to the soul. Then he marked her with a rhythm there that took her breath, even through their layers of clothing.

"Too many clothes," he murmured as the rubbing was no longer enough, breaking off his assault of her mouth and sitting back on his knees. His gaze raked across her and anticipation rippled over her skin. She arched her back as his fingers released her buttons, parting the sides of her blouse. He ran a single finger down her cleavage, straight to her navel, then moved back up to flick open the front clasp on her bra. It fell away from her breasts, leaving them exposed...to his eyes, to his hands—she closed her eyes as they cupped her, molding them in his fingers—and then... Oh glory. To his mouth. His tongue laved over the first crest, pulling it into his mouth while darts of *something* shot straight to her core, ripping a groan from her throat. Oh God. He smiled against her flesh and she could hardly breathe. She heard a soft chuckle, like he knew exactly what he was doing to her. She didn't care. If anything, it made the air seem hotter. And when he moved to the other breast and ran his tongue over the nipple there, she cried out with the thrill of it.

His mouth found hers again, briefly stamping it with possession. "God Ell, you're still so sweet," he whispered hotly in her ear. "Are you this sweet...everywhere?"

He slid down her body, stopping for a moment to kiss her navel, and she felt his breath, hot against her jeans. He reached for the button and slid the zipper down with a minimum of fuss. He pulled the whole lot down her legs—jeans and the scrap of fabric that could just be termed underwear in the tiniest, most miniscule sense. Dropping them on the floor, he took a moment to simply look at her. Her muscles tensed almost painfully in response to the path of his gaze.

At the first touch of his mouth to her flesh, she twisted on the bed, driven crazy by the sensation of his smooth tongue against her. Memories slammed into her, one after another, mixing with tantalizing sensations from the here and now. The soft ruffles of his hair tickled the insides of her thighs as his gentle assault undid her inch by inch. Her fingers slid down her body to tangle with his hair as she pressed her feet into the mattress, lifting herself higher in response to the waves of pleasure rocking through her. Waves that turned to a pounding surf of intense need as with one long, delectable stroke of his tongue he sent her crashing over the edge. The spasms drew a long, keening cry from her lips, ending with his name as her legs went utterly limp.

Dev looked up at her face as she melted in his hands. Her blonde curls were spread in a tangle on the pillow, her lashes lay on her cheeks as, with eyes closed, she fought for breath. Her breasts rose and fell with each tortured rhythm, her blouse still gaping open—the only scrap of clothing on the bed. The lamplight glowed off the sheen of her skin, the peaks of her breasts erect, tempting. He closed his eyes, fighting the need to take her right here and now, roughly.

He'd wanted to hear his name on her lips, and he had. But it wasn't enough. He wanted it to last.

He slid off the bed, slowly undid his zipper and stripped off his jeans and shorts. Ella's eyes opened, heavy lidded, and she smiled like a cat that had got the cream. Never had she been more beautiful, except perhaps when she'd looked at him with the same sort of exhausted wonder on their wedding night.

She reached out and circled him with her hand, and he lost the ability to think. All he knew was that he wanted her. Needed her. And tonight he'd have her. The rest he'd deal with later.

Her fingers felt so damn good. Firmly yet slowly, she stroked. But there was only so much a man could take. He pressed her back into the pillows, parting her legs and sliding inside her with one sure stroke.

And froze as their gazes caught, and the gravity of what had just happened struck them both. His arms trembled not from his weight but from fear, emotion, need. He'd nearly given up that he'd be here again, buried inside her, feeling the warmth of her surrounding him. It was as close to heaven as he was ever going to get. It was more than a meeting of bodies. It always had been. And yet the primal, physical need raged through him.

Her muscles clenched and he struggled, wanting to hold on, make it last longer. In the end he lost and took on a rhythm that was as natural, as graceful to him as a fly-cast—a smooth long stroke, a small retreat, and extending again...and again, and again. His pace quickened as her fingernails raked along the skin of his back, her gasps of pleasure an aphrodisiac as his heart pounded through every pore of his skin.

She cried out a second time and he was indestructible.

And then he answered with her name on his lips and he was destroyed.

Chapter Six

He was still sleeping, his lashes lying against his cheeks, when she opened her eyes.

The previous night came back crystal clear, sending a flush over her body. This time she couldn't blame it on the alcohol. This time she'd had a choice. She could say for old times' sake until she was blue in the face. The truth was she'd wanted him. She'd wanted every square inch of him and that was exactly what she'd gotten. And then some.

When his hands had been on her skin and her name on his lips, nothing else existed. But now, in the washed-out light of a cloudy fall morning, everything existed. She'd been swayed by his generosity towards a sick woman, seduced by memories and entranced by his sexiness. She'd let it all get to her and this was where they'd ended up.

But she knew last night was meaningless in the overall scheme of things. This wasn't what she wanted, and so it changed nothing. She couldn't live here, like this. She'd resent him before a month was out.

Why couldn't he just change? She slipped out from between the sheets and silently grappled for some clothes. She knew everyone—whoever everyone was—said asking a person to change was impossible. But really. If he'd just show a little effort, a little motivation. She wasn't asking perfection.

Just...different. Didn't he have *goals*? Didn't he want more?

"Going somewhere?"

His first words of the morning came out rough and raspy and unbearably sexy. She knew beneath the sheet he was stark naked and the muscles between her legs involuntarily tightened in a simple yet effective reaction.

But one thing about waking the morning after stuck. This—no matter how mind-blowing it was—wasn't enough. It never had been.

"I have to get back to Denver, remember?"

He sat up against the pillows, watching her every move. Feeling exposed was silly, considering. But she did and she hurriedly stepped into underwear and jeans, did without her bra and pulled on an old sweatshirt of his that was lying on a chair, simply to cover her naked breasts.

"So you're still going."

"Of course I am."

His chin flattened and she braced herself for another argument.

"You really want this divorce, don't you, Ella?"

His eyes were inscrutable, and yet she thought she heard the teeniest bit of regret in his voice. But why would he regret it? He'd never attempted to save their marriage, and he'd had a decade of opportunities. He'd never come after her, never returned her earlier decrees in person. She'd geared herself up for a fight for her independence, but he'd never so much as communicated a single syllable. Up until this weekend he hadn't made any demands on her at all.

And the moment he had, she'd fallen straight into his bed. Maybe she should count her lucky stars that he hadn't pressed the issue all those years ago. She probably wouldn't have been strong enough to resist him. Her life would have turned out very differently—she would have left school and her aspirations behind. She was damned well going to be strong enough now.

"Yes," she said clearly, "I do. I stayed the weekend, Dev. I held up my end. Now it's time for you to hold up yours. Let me go. Let me go home and write Betty's story. Let me get on with my life." Her words were sincere even as they left a sinking feeling in the pit of her stomach.

"Isn't that what you've been doing?"

The truth of that stung and she stalked out the door and down the hall to the kitchen. Her bag sat, already packed yesterday, at the end of the couch. The typewriter was in its battered case on the coffee table beside it. It was the only thing she really wanted to take with her. The rest could stay. Including Devin.

She heard him stumping his way down the hall and braced herself. She needed to be firm now. Nothing had changed just because they'd made love. They'd agreed it was one last time, a farewell to their marriage. It had to stay that way. Squaring her shoulders, she exhaled and turned around.

He'd followed her down the hall with the bed sheet gathered up and wrapped low around his hips. The rest of him—every glorious inch of his arms and chest—was naked. Even though Ella knew she was leaving, her fingers itched to touch him. To know him again.

Sexual attraction. More than attraction. *Need. It isn't enough*, she reminded herself.

"Do you need a pen?" She said it and lifted her chin, challenging.

"Let me check my pocket... Oops, I guess not," he replied slowly, the grin that crawled up his cheek holding an edge of sarcasm. He held the cotton sheet with one hand. A corner had begun to droop and she wet her lips. She couldn't let him drop that sheet.

She grabbed her purse and drew out a pen, then took the papers from the envelope and thrust them into his free hand.

"Dammit, Ella—"

"Don't dammit me. I'll put my things in the car. When I come back, it would be great if you could have those ready to go." She angled her head, gesturing towards the papers in his hand.

His lips curled and she knew he was on the verge of resisting. But he had to do this for her. She had to go back to Denver. She had to leave him behind and forget they'd ever been married.

"Devin. What do you really expect? Did you think I'd change my mind in a weekend? Did you think I'd try to turn back the clock and I'd go back to living this way? It's not who I am anymore. I'm glad I saw you. I might be glad you forced me into a goodbye, because we never had one before. I'm even glad we had sex." She aimed a sly smile at him, meant to melt his resistance, lighten the atmosphere. "I mean, it's hard not to be grateful."

"Ell," he said, softer, and she could see he was on the verge of speaking. She knew that whatever it was, it would be something she didn't want to hear.

"Please, Devin," she pleaded softly, her throat thickening. He was so *everything* when he forgot about the chip on his shoulder for five seconds. "I can't go on this way."

Everything held for a long moment. Dev met her gaze and she had the absurd urge to go to him, wrap herself in his arms and tell him she didn't mean it. Memories washed over her, of falling in love with him the first time and the rebirth of those feelings even though it was wrong. And a sense of finality. She waited for him to accept it.

He looked away first.

"Go load the car," he relented softly.

Her carefully held breath came out in a sigh of relief as she put her bag over her shoulder and picked up the typewriter. "Thank you."

When she had stowed her bag, she went in one last time for the papers. He held the envelope out to her, the pen hooked on the top of the Tyvek rectangle. The backs of her eyes stung when she took them from his hand. It was what she wanted, right? Then why the hell didn't she feel any relief, like she expected?

He stepped forward, hooked his free arm around her and dragged her close.

His lips met hers, a furious clash of anger and apology and love that cut her off at the knees. He lifted his other hand and cupped her face, dropping the sheet negligently to the floor. With a strangled cry, she pushed away, wrenching herself out of his arms and refusing to look at him standing there, like an avenging god, in the tiny shack she somehow would always think of as home.

She stumbled out the door and into her car. And left in a cloud of dust that lingered not nearly as long as the taste of him on her lips.

"Come on. That's prime real estate right there, Ella." Amy sipped on her pomegranate martini and angled a freshly waxed eyebrow in the direction of the hot guy leaning over the bar. "Look at that ass. You could bounce quarters off it."

Ella sighed and used the straw to toy with the slice of lemon in her tonic water. It was the only thing that seemed to appeal tonight. And that included the tall, dark and not-so-dangerous metrosexual picking up a martini at the bar.

She'd only spent forty-eight hours with Devin, but Ella knew she preferred his rough-and-ready sexiness to the immaculate appearance of the man Amy couldn't seem to drag her eyes away from.

"So go for it, Ames."

"Uh uh. This is *your* night." She sipped her drink again, then tossed her curls over her shoulder. "Your article was a smash hit. Hell, Donovan's asked for a follow-up. To celebrate you should definitely hook up. I mean, how long has it been? You deserve some fun. And that could be some serious fun." Amy angled her face up alluringly as the man passed by their table carrying two drinks. Ella didn't miss how his eyes lingered on her friend's long expanse of leg, barely capped by the scandalously short leather skirt she wore.

Maybe not so much Ella's type—at the moment—but the look in his eyes had definitely been hungry. Just weeks ago Dev had looked at her the same way. There was a marked difference between this polished club and the rowdiness of the saloon in Durango. But one thing remained the same, not matter what the atmosphere—the mating ritual. And Ella wasn't interested in playing the game. Not anymore.

After leaving the cabin that Sunday she'd returned to her apartment. She'd shed significant tears during the long drive, only to have them turn hot with anger when she realized he'd given her the papers back *unsigned.*

She'd called him several unladylike names in sequence. Devin had backed her into a corner. She had work to hand in and no time to go back. She hadn't even told Amy the divorce papers weren't filed. She wasn't quite sure how to explain it. How to explain that in one weekend of mind-blowing sex he'd managed to make a complete marshmallow of her. She'd temporarily forgotten her focus. She'd ignored every voice in her head that told her to stand her ground, and she'd succumbed to the fierce desire she felt simply by breathing the same air as he did. One night. All it took was one single night. And while she wouldn't admit it to another living soul, she knew the problem.

She missed him again.

The stress had to be getting to her. She wasn't sleeping, wasn't eating and was so tired during the day because of it that she kept dozing off before she even got dinner ready for herself.

Now the powers that be wanted her to follow Betty's story through to the end...and today she'd come up with a doozy of a revelation in her research. Devin wasn't who she thought. He hadn't been for many, many years. He'd lied to her that weekend at the cabin. And he'd made a fool of her, first by letting her believe he hadn't changed and second by making sure they were still married.

All of it simply exhausted her.

"I'm sorry, Ames, you're gonna have to fly solo," she apologized. "I'm wiped.

"You're tired all the time lately," Amy complained, toying with her cocktail napkin, annoyed. "I practically had to drag you out tonight."

"I know. I guess I've been working a lot."

"No more than usual," she observed. "And you turned your nose up at the veal piccata earlier too, and it's your favorite." Amy's eyes deepened with worry. "Are you sure you're not sick, Ell?"

Ella stirred the slice of lemon in her plain tonic water. Even tonight, the thought of the usual celebratory lemon drop martinis—her favorite—turned her off. Maybe she was coming down with something. She hadn't been sick, but nothing seemed to appeal lately.

"I don't know. Is there a flu going around?"

But Amy shook her head. "You've been off for a couple of weeks now. Longer than a flu. You haven't been the same since you got back from Durango."

Durango. A flash of recognition flared through her before settling, icy cold, in the pit of her stomach.

She hadn't been the same since being with Devin.

She was tired and her appetite was off.

As numbness spread over her limbs, she counted days. Oh. My. God.

"Ella? God, you're not going to be sick are you?" The good-looking prey was forgotten as Amy clasped Ella's cold hand.

"Durango," she whispered hoarsely.

Her voice was drowned out by the rhythmic thump thump of the music, but Amy saw her form the word. "Durango?" It took little time for her friend to put it together. "Devin? Damn, Ella. Did you sleep with your ex-husband?"

A few heads turned and Ella felt her cheeks flare. "Can we get out of here?"

Without a word Amy grabbed her tiny purse and slid out from behind the table. They grabbed their coats at the check and stepped out into the brisk fall air.

Ella went to a nearby bench, sat and leaned forward, putting her head between her knees. She sucked in the cool, sweet air as her mind raced. It wasn't possible. It had been one night. She couldn't have been so stupid...

Of course not. It couldn't be. She was just run down, that was all. Surely she wouldn't be feeling this way so soon. It took weeks to feel symptoms, didn't it? It could just be stress. She'd been working hard first at the article for the paper and then putting together a portfolio for the Boston job. She breathed deeply, feeling the moment of cloying dizziness pass. She had been working too hard and not eating enough. That was all. She was run down, just like she'd said.

Amy sat beside her on the bench and put a hand on her shoulder. "Are you pregnant, Ell?" She said it softly, without the shock and hint of judgment that had been in her voice inside the club. Tears stung the backs of Ella's eyes. She couldn't be pregnant. She was just planning on starting another chapter in her life. And a baby wasn't on the agenda.

"I don't know," she whispered back, horrified at how unsettled her voice seemed.

"Are you late?"

With a huge lump in her throat, Ella nodded. "About a week or so."

"You haven't done a test?"

"It never crossed my mind until tonight."

Ella sat back on the bench and covered her mouth with a hand. She slid her fingers over her chin and closed her eyes. There was no possible way. It would be an unmitigated disaster. "Amy, I can't be pregnant. I can't."

"Did you sleep with Devin?"

She nodded, eyes still closed.

Amy was silent for a few moments before saying knowingly, "Then I'm afraid, Ella, you can."

The idea terrified her. She lowered her hand and rested it against her belly. Was it possible that after all this time she was carrying Devin's child? The irony wasn't lost on her. She'd run away to avoid this very thing—being tied down with a family, no way out. And now, just as she'd thought she was close to getting everything she wanted...

Devin's baby.

"Let's not panic quite yet," Amy advised. "Let's get a test first. We'll go back to your apartment and I'll stay with you, okay?"

Ella looked over at Amy. Amy had used hot rollers to put gorgeous curls in her brown hair, then left it to cascade onto her shoulders. Her leather skirt was short and the halter top beyond sexy. Amy always looked like she belonged in a fashion magazine. But what Ella really saw at this moment was a friend. A friend that she needed very badly.

"I'd like that," Ella admitted, standing and taking a breath to fight off the weakness she felt in her limbs.

They grabbed a cab and Ella waited while Amy dashed into a drugstore for the test. When she came back out, they drove the rest of the way to Ella's apartment in silence. Ella paid the cab driver and took out her keys.

Amy didn't know Ella and Devin weren't divorced. Amy also didn't know the shocking bit of news that Ella had uncovered today. Devin wasn't who he seemed. Oh no, he was much, much more. He wasn't the man she knew at all. She'd read through the information with a sinking heart—ending with the recent article in *Colorado Entrepreneur*. She'd been played. And she was still married to him. Possibly carrying his child. Panic threaded through her. She'd accused Devin of many things, but he'd never been deceitful. Until now. How could she trust him with anything? Why had he done it?

"Have you taken one of these things before?" Amy asked as she dropped the shopping bag on the dining table.

Ella shook her head, trying to wrestle her thoughts to the present. There had never been any need for pregnancy tests before. Despite dating occasionally, she hadn't actually been with anyone other than Dev. She knew Amy would be shocked at that tidbit of information. In this day and age it was inconceivable that she'd been celibate for this long. But without being officially free, she couldn't bring herself to take things to a sexual level, not and keep a clear conscience. She'd made her own life, but being married to Dev had held her back in ways he probably hadn't imagined.

"Okay." Amy opened the box. "Basically, you pee on this end. Then you wait."

Ella's hand shook as she took the test and stared at the blank spot. "And if I am?"

"One line you're in the clear. Two lines and we're shopping for teddy bears."

Ella looked up into Amy's solemn brown eyes.

"Ell, I'll be here for you no matter what, okay?"

Ella gave Amy a quick hug. "I'd better go do this."

She went into the bathroom, locked the door and tried to catch her breath. Pregnant. It wasn't possible. The test would prove it. The next time she saw Dev, it would be to get the truth. All of the truth.

The minutes ticked by, but before the big hand hit the seven on her watch, she already knew.

Blinking past the stinging at the backs of her eyes, she opened the bathroom door and held the stick out to Amy.

"Congratulations," Amy said quietly.

Ella's briefcase doubled as carry on baggage as she stepped off the commuter plane. Inside was her laptop, notebooks and pens, chargers for both laptop and cell phone. In addition was a small clear bag with makeup essentials, clean underwear, a spare pair of pantyhose and one bottle of prenatal vitamins.

Her stomach churned as she stepped across the tarmac towards the entrance. It had nothing to do with the breakfast she'd eaten before departure. Nope. It had everything to do with seeing Devin again. And once again, having to combine work with a personal errand.

This time he had to sign the papers.

She picked up her rental car and drove straight downtown to the address she'd entered in her PDA. This was a different area of town from where she had visited last time. Not the rough edges of Ruby Shoes saloon or the small, weathered cabin where she and Devin had spent the weekend. Durango was small town, but the core had been revitalized in recent years. She parked on the street outside one of the many brick, square-fronted buildings. In younger years it had been home to a real estate company and legal office. Now it housed DMQ Properties. Devin's business. The venture she'd known nothing about until she'd been researching Betty's case for the follow-up article. Why had he kept it a secret? What kind of head game was he playing? Or had he simply taken pleasure in making a fool of her?

For several minutes she stayed in the car, measuring her breaths and collecting her thoughts. She had been so determined to leave Dev behind that she'd locked away any curiosity, flatly refusing to use her resources to check up on him. She didn't want to know where he was or what he was doing. That's what shutting the door on an old life meant. No moments of weakness. No wondering what if. Just a clean slate.

She'd never guessed she'd run into him on an assignment years later. Or how involved he'd actually *be* in that assignment. She'd failed to do her research out of some sense of self-preservation and now she looked incompetent.

Now here he was, up to his eyeballs in Betty's plight and her job relied on her following the trail where it led. Her boss had made it clear—he'd been like a dog with a bone. He wanted a follow-up article *yesterday*. The paper had even sprung for her flight and rental expense, something they hadn't done before.

At the heart of it all was Devin. The cabin was not his home, the ranch not his work. He had a condo overlooking the mountains and a thriving company. He was rich. Far more than they'd ever dreamed while lying in the field and counting stars at night. Stinking rich. Rich enough that Betty Tucker had no more medical bills to worry about—they had been paid in full. How many other people had he fooled? Why hadn't he just paid for her treatment from the beginning?

There were so many questions he had to answer. But most of all her pride hurt. He'd deliberately let her believe he hadn't changed...all the while seducing her with his sexy grin and bedroom eyes. Knowing which buttons to push. Laughing at her.

She blinked furiously at the angry tears that gathered in the corners of her eyes. She would not cry about Devin McQuade ever again. She would not let anyone make her a laughingstock ever again. She would not be played for a fool.

Ella pressed her hand to her still-flat tummy. It seemed impossible that there were such life-altering changes going on inside when outwardly she looked exactly the same. That this one thing was happening to her while the rest of the world was spinning out of control.

Ella closed her eyes, seeing Devin's face behind her lids. Smiling. Laughing. Darkly intense in the moment before he kissed her.

If he knew about the baby he would never sign the divorce

decree. And time was running out. If he didn't sign them this trip, she'd either have to go through this all again, or go in front of a judge and try for an uncontested divorce. And if Devin knew about the baby there'd be a whole lot of contesting going on. He'd never give up his own child without a fight. The last thing she wanted was an ugly court battle.

Opening her eyes, Ella filled herself with all the resolve she'd been storing up for days. She would talk to Devin. She would get her answers and her divorce. He'd kept enough secrets from her. She was entitled to a few of her own.

But the mere thought of deceiving him didn't sit well with her conscience. What was good for the goose wasn't necessarily good for the gander after all. And this was a child. She knew she couldn't go through the rest of her life denying Devin the knowledge of his own son or daughter. She would tell him.

But later. When she was used to the idea, when she had a plan. She had to believe it would all fall into place. She grabbed the handles of the briefcase and shut the car door firmly.

The reception area of DMQ Properties was welcoming, quiet and professional. The walls were a restful taupe with wide white trim. The reception desk was dark wood with a frosted glass wall behind it. Ella could see the bulky shadows of filing cabinets and a copy machine through the frosted glass. A woman in perhaps her mid-forties sat behind the desk, her wire glasses perched on her nose.

"Ella...Turner for Mr. McQuade," Ella announced herself at the desk.

The woman looked down her spectacles while simultaneously raising her gaze to Ella's. It resulted with Ella being made to feel like a disobedient school girl. She pushed a polite smile onto her lips. "I believe he's expecting me," she added.

The receptionist's smile was more a false gritting of teeth than a genuine expression of pleasure. "Please have a seat," she suggested, before disappearing down a short hall.

Ella sat in one of the padded chairs, placing her briefcase beside her on the floor. The tailored skirt and jacket she wore had once been a confidence builder and now felt tight and cloying. Already her figure was changing in small, invisible ways.

The phone rang and the receptionist returned to her desk, answering and swiveling in her chair as she reached for a file. Ella looked around her. It was impossible to believe Devin owned this. Impossible to believe he hadn't mentioned it during their time together only a few short weeks earlier.

"Ella. Please come in."

Her lashes snapped up and she saw Devin standing next to the reception desk. She fought to keep her expression bland, but it was a struggle. This man was as familiar to her as breathing, each inch of his flesh imprinted on her memory. Yet today he seemed a stranger in a charcoal gray suit. He wore no tie, and his white shirt was unbuttoned at the top. Ella wet her lips as she rose, grabbing the handles of her case. Without a word to the receptionist, she followed Devin down the hall to his office, her heels echoing on the floor with each step.

Once inside, he immediately went back to his desk and sat, without pleasantries, without waiting for her to be seated first. Ella ignored the snub and went to stand before his desk, raising one eyebrow as his gaze flickered over her. He leaned back in his leather chair. "I suppose you've brought the papers back."

A cold, impersonal smile touched just the corners of her lips. "You lied to me. You never signed them as you said you would."

"Maybe I wasn't ready to let you go after our weekend

together."

He ran a finger along his lower lip. The gesture made Ella's blood simmer with anger. He was playing games, and she didn't like it one bit. She'd put up with their weekend together, and she'd played by his rules. A little too well, she remembered, resisting the urge to touch her belly once more. But she was done playing games. He'd made her a bargain and then he'd failed to deliver on his part. He would sign the papers today. She should have done as her lawyer suggested and gone through the courts from the beginning. She was kicking herself for it now. The last thing she wanted to do was wait for a court date so long that her...condition...would be readily apparent.

"Ready or not, we had a deal and you didn't keep it. I hope you honor your business agreements better than your personal ones."

The finger stopped moving and his eyes darkened. "Be careful, Ella," he replied softly. "Marriage is also a legal agreement, and one that you didn't honor in the least."

The blood rushed out of her face. Little did he know how much she actually had been faithful to their marriage. "I have never moved on. Not in the way you think. It's one of the reasons I want to make it official."

"What do you mean, never moved on? You managed to make it like I never existed."

Her gaze was drawn to the slight sneer of his lips. Is that what made him angry? Thinking she'd forgotten him? Because she'd tried. She really, really had.

"I never pretended you didn't exist."

He didn't respond immediately, instead letting the silence speak for him. In those moments she could almost hear his thoughts. Knew the last part had been a lie.

"Yes, you did," he said finally. "I was something you swept

under the rug. An inconvenience to your professional life. A dirty secret. Tell me," he said bitterly, "did it also inconvenience your sex life? Having a paper husband?"

She felt the heat rise up her neck. He could think a lot of things about her, and many of them would be true. But the one thing she hadn't done was sleep around. "What sex life?" she challenged quietly.

Devin stood from his chair. "You mean you haven't slept with a single man since leaving me high and dry? I don't believe you." His voice ground out the words, and she heard the underlying skepticism.

She was guilty of a lot of things, but this wasn't one of them.

"That's exactly what I'm saying. Whether or not you believe me is up to you."

He made a disbelieving noise in the back of his throat as he leaned his hands on the desk. "You promised me a hell of a lot more than your fidelity. Love. Honor. Cherish." His lips twisted and she swore there was something that resembled pain in his eyes. "Better or worse," he continued. "Richer or poorer. Sickness and health. Do you remember those?"

"And you haven't kept a thing hidden from me over the years? What about all this?" She swept her hand out, encompassing his office. One wall was almost completely windows, looking out over the sharp relief of the hills. "You didn't tell me about DMQ. You let me believe you were the same old Devin." Her voice rose and her breath caught. "You don't run the old place at all, do you? You don't even live there."

It made sense. The old furniture, the nearly empty cupboards. It was still his, but it wasn't his home. The moment she'd realized it she'd felt so stupid. As Ella confronted him, those feelings came rushing back. It was humiliating.

"Sit down. You're getting worked up."

She thought of the biggest lie of all standing between them and sank weakly into the chair. She'd wanted to keep this cool, business-like. And within seconds the whole situation had flared into a passionate *he said she said.* Exactly what she hadn't wanted.

"You also didn't tell me you were planning on paying all of Betty's medical bills." She took a deep breath, let it out. Felt pleased at how her last sentence had come out just as she intended. Cold, professional and skewering him to the spot. The brief look of surprise in his eyes spoke volumes. "You never wanted me to know, did you?"

"I never intended for *anyone* to find out. That was a private matter." His jaw tightened.

She smiled smugly. "Then you should have covered your tracks better. Why didn't you just pay her bill? Why the benefit?"

Devin sighed. "Because I understand something that you never have. There is a community here. People band together. My lawyer was handling the legal part with the HMO. The benefit was supposed to help Betty with some of her expenses."

Ella shook off the feeling of being chastised and focused on the issue at hand. "But?"

"But the legal channels were taking too long and Betty needed to start her treatment. The few thousand we raised is a drop in the bucket, you know that. So I paid for her chemotherapy." He sent her a hard stare. "Anonymously."

Devin regarded her for several seconds, and that slow turning returned to her stomach. A teasing or even angry Devin she knew how to deal with. But he was neither of those things right now. He was calculating. In control.

"Nothing is truly anonymous if you know where to look."

He gave a small, satisfied smile and resumed his seat. "Exactly. I didn't realize my finances were going to be examined quite so closely. You found out about Betty, but you didn't know I owned DMQ? Do you honestly expect me to believe that?"

Of course he would pick up on her mistake. The truth was she hadn't *wanted* to know. She hadn't wanted to see how Devin was living without her. It was easier to think of him still at the cabin. Easier to think of him exactly as she'd found him that night at Ruby Shoes. It made her decisions feel that much more justified. So while she'd done scads of research during her degree and now for her job, the topic of Devin was one she left very much alone. That denial was coming back to bite her in the ass...big time.

"Wow, you really do have an ego, don't you?" She flashed a smart-aleck smile that she didn't feel. "I didn't have any reason to check up on you. We were *over*. If I hadn't been looking into Betty's story, I wouldn't have known a thing. Your little deception last weekend would never have been discovered."

"And are you disappointed?"

She wrinkled her brow. "What do you mean?"

He rocked back in his chair, tossed his pen down on a blotter. "It was easier to think of me being that deadbeat, wasn't it?"

That he could still see inside her thoughts as clearly as he always had was disconcerting. "You're talking nonsense."

"Oh come on. You made it perfectly clear when you bought me in that auction. You thought I was still on the ranch, thought I still lived in that tiny place content with a beer and a ball game."

Ella had the grace to blush. It was exactly what she'd thought.

He rose from his chair and came around the desk. "You never did give me enough credit, Ella. DMQ is mine. I decided building wasn't enough. I wanted to own the properties I was building."

"It's obviously working for you."

He stood in front of her, close enough she could smell his aftershave, their bodies only inches apart. It was like a hit to the gut, the scent taking her back a mere few weeks to the cabin and being held against his muscled, bare chest. Her breasts peaked in response and she was at once grateful for the dark blazer hiding the evidence.

"Tell me something," he murmured, his voice silky in the quiet of the office. "Am I more attractive to you now that you know I have money?"

Ella bit down on her lip, unbearably turned on by his nearness and abashed by his accusation. "That's not it," she tried, but knew it came out sounding shallow and insincere.

"Does it help to know I'm a millionaire? Does that make me irresistible? Do you still want a divorce now? Or are you back for half of everything?"

He took a step closer and she swallowed. Her body was going into overdrive just having him this near. What was it about him that kept her wanting more? That made her forget all the reasons why they were wrong for each other and simply crave the feeling of his body pressed against hers?

"Dev, don't..." The protest came out weakly. Dear God, she'd come as a last chance to get his signature, and she was carrying his child. How could she possibly...

Devin erased all thoughts from her mind as he took the last step in, the lapels of his jacket brushing seductively against the tips of her breasts as her breathing labored. His gaze burned into hers and his lips parted. She wanted those lips on hers.

She wanted them everywhere. The muscles between her legs clenched in anticipation as his gaze slid down her face to the V in her blazer, focusing on the shadowed hint of cleavage.

"Does knowing I have a condo overlooking the mountains, one with a very large, very plush bed, make it easier to accept?"

For a breath, the words seemed to lodge in her throat. Both their chests rose and fell like runaway trains, straining against endless buttons. "Make what easier to accept?" she finally got out, the words sounding squeezed.

His gaze rose, clashed with hers once more. "This," he growled, then reached out and pulled her flush against his body, his mouth meeting hers in a grand explosion of passion.

Chapter Seven

Devin felt her soft lips open beneath his and his blood surged. He hadn't been able to erase her from his mind since the morning she'd gone back to Denver. He woke in the night, aroused and in a sweat from seeing her in his dreams. When he'd checked the appointments this morning on his BlackBerry, he'd been darkly pleased to see Ella's name scheduled in.

It was all working the way he'd wanted for the most part. He knew by not signing the papers he was forcing her hand, ensuring she'd be back. And this time he'd be in control of the situation rather than on the wrong foot. She was unable to avoid the truth any longer—that she'd made a big mistake leaving him behind all those years ago. Now she could see him for who he truly was. What he'd made of himself. What he'd promised her if she'd only be patient. He'd done exactly as he'd said he would, only she hadn't had faith in him.

He was torn between wanting to rub her nose in it and wanting to ignore it all in favor of another chance in her eyes. How was it that one taste of her made him forget all the reasons why he should still hate her?

Her sun-streaked blonde hair was up in a tidy, professional coil, and he blindly felt with his fingertips, pulling out pins and dropping them carelessly on the floor as he kissed her. The mass of gold fell over his hands, the floral scent of vanilla and jasmine rising from the strands as he twined her hair around his fingers.

She'd haunted his thoughts day and night ever since the auction at Ruby's when he'd seen her standing there looking like a fish out of water. In her slim skirt and expensive blouse, sipping on ice water and looking like she was above it all. All he could think about was unwrapping the layers, trying to get to the girl he'd fallen in love with.

And now she was here, just like he knew she'd be. One more layer peeled away.

She moaned into his mouth and his pulse leapt. He wanted her so much it was becoming hugely uncomfortable. The fireworks exploding between them were stronger than ever. The night at the cabin had proved that. Had she truly thought he could let her walk away after they'd made love again? After he'd felt her, tasted her, heard her sigh his name in the dark?

No damn way. It had moved well past revenge now. He'd known she was leaving, but he did the one thing he knew would ensure her return. He didn't sign the decree. He wasn't the idealistic boy she'd married. This time he'd fight for Ella, and this time it would be on his terms. He wasn't young, poor and helpless any longer.

His fingers found the buttons of her blazer and he turned them, feeling the thick material fall away as it gaped open. Beneath it she wore a navy silk camisole, soft and sultry. Tiny spaghetti straps held it up, but they were superfluous. Her breasts were rising and falling rapidly with her increased breaths, the peaked nipples straining against the fabric as he covered them with his palms.

Ella pulled away from his kiss, her eyes wide with denial. "No Dev...I didn't come here for this..."

It wasn't fear he saw in the blue depths of her gaze. It was uncertainty. And longing. And something else...guilt? He was on good terms with guilt—it was easy to recognize. But what did she have to feel guilty about?

"Then why did you come?" Devin kept his voice soft, seductive, and moved back slightly. He gentled his hands, teasing the tips of her breasts with his fingers. She released a gratifying, shaky breath.

"To get the story..." Her eyes slid closed.

So it wasn't all about the papers. Or she was covering? Either way, at this moment she wasn't focused on the divorce. He slid his hand over the curve of her bottom, smiled at her gasp as he drew her close against him. He knew she was focused on exactly the same thing he was. The intense passion between them that had never disappeared.

He moved to the door and flicked the lock, wasting no time. There was no way he wanted to kill the moment. He'd waited years for her to come back. He'd exacted his pound of flesh at the cabin and it had left him unsatisfied. Only holding her in his arms had given any relief. Now he had something to prove— to her, and to himself.

There was no room now for revenge or playing games. This was want, pure and simple. A lust so strong he had only ever felt it for *one* woman. Ella.

When he returned to her, she was scrambling to button the blazer.

"Don't," he commanded, and her hands fell still.

"I can't do this," she whispered, and the words somehow reached in and touched his heart.

"You don't want to? Because you know I'd never force you, Ella." He ran his hand over her hip, grazing her bottom, loving the feel of her in the tidy little skirt. "You say when. You say how far this goes. You know that."

He hooked a tiny strap around his baby finger. "Your skin is as soft as the silk," he murmured. But he waited. He could be a very patient man. Years of necessity had taught him how, and then it had paid off in more ways than he'd expected. He'd stayed the course and it had made him a very rich man. He could be patient with Ella too. It didn't mean he was above being persuasive. Not when he knew it was what they both wanted. "I want to touch it, you know. Your skin. All of it."

"Why, Dev?" Ella ran her tongue over her lips. "Why now?"

"You haven't guessed?"

She shook her head, the blonde cascade of hair falling over her shoulders. God, she was beautiful. The need to get back at her for the past faded away, leaving him shaking with the truth. He still loved his wife. Or at least the woman he'd married. But he couldn't bring himself to say it. There was such a thing as too much honesty, and he didn't want to hear her denials or have his words handed back to him.

"The last time wasn't nearly enough. I want you so much it's killing me not to be inside you right now."

The words seemed to shimmer in the air.

"But if that's not what I want?"

It if wasn't what she wanted, he'd back off. It'd damn near do him in, but he'd do it. He wanted her to come to him of her own free will.

"Is it what you want?"

Silence fell in the room. "We're in your office," she whispered, but he heard the temptation in her voice. He knew she was on the verge of giving in and the blood in his veins pulsed faster.

"I don't give a damn where we are. Do you? The door's locked." He caught her gaze with his, let his lips curve up in a conspiratorial grin. "My schedule is open until lunch."

Ella's body was going into overdrive and she was fighting as best she knew how. She was here to gather information. But she'd never been able to resist him. It was one of the reasons she'd had to make a clean break. Being near him would have ruined all her plans. It would have muddied the waters. Made her lose her focus.

Like it was now.

But she wanted him, so badly her body was weeping for his touch. The door was locked, and the look in his eyes was electrifying. The memory of how good it was between them refused to fade into the background. There was something forbidden and illicit about his office that excited her.

Goosebumps erupted on her skin as he touched her. What would happen when he found out about the baby? He'd hate her all over again. With his hands on her body and his smooth voice playing devil's advocate, she weakened, wanting one last time with him before it all blew up. She was like a Devin addict, swearing each time that this was the last one and then succumbing to him all over again.

"Ella," he murmured, and his fingers grazed the tips of her breasts once more. A rush of desire settled between her legs, hot and wet.

She reached out for his suit jacket and pushed it off his shoulders. It fell to the floor where it would surely crease, but with her hands on him neither of them seemed to care. Her fingers trembled—with anticipation, not fear—as she undid the buttons of his shirt, pulling the tails out of his trousers. Finally, finally, she touched the warmth of his chest, her fingertips playing over the smooth skin. At this moment she didn't see him as the enemy. Maybe she should. Maybe then common sense would outweigh the elemental excitement from touching him and having him touch her. But it was more than that. As his fingers unzipped her skirt and pushed it down over her hips, she realized she was about to make love to the father of her child.

And as her heart stuttered over the enormity of that fact, she was hit with another.

It *would* be making love. Because she had never stopped loving Devin McQuade. And it was a damnable thing to love a man you were determined to divorce.

Her skin broke out in goosebumps again as he stepped away from her, the heat of his body suddenly absent. She stood before him, dressed in only her navy camisole and matching silk panties, sheer stockings and her favorite silver heels.

"You are more beautiful now than you ever were," he murmured, staring. "I didn't think it was possible."

The words sat on her tongue, begging to be said. That there was a tiny life inside of her that was his. But in all the chaos created by her libido, she was at least clear-headed enough to know he still needed to let her go, and he wouldn't if he knew she were pregnant. She would not lose herself in him once again. She'd seen enough of that as a child, seeing her mother fall deeply in love, molding herself to her lovers' expectations only to be abandoned within months.

Marrying Devin had been a mistake, a reaction to a terrible time. She'd been too lonely, too idealistic to see it for what it was. Now it was a one hundred and eighty degree turn. Dev was a highly successful, single businessman. A wife and a baby... She knew her own aspirations would count for nothing. He would expect her to play a supportive role. For him to go from nothing to this... She had been around enough to know how many hours of work that took. He wouldn't give it up.

There was no room for her here. Not without sacrificing all

her dreams and hopes for the future.

So she hugged the secret to herself, wanting, needing, to feel that closeness one last time before their marriage ended one way or another.

"Make love to me, Dev."

He didn't need a second invitation. He came forward, the incorrigible smile she adored dawning once again, his body pushing her backwards until her bottom lightly hit the edge of his desk.

She reached for his belt at the same time as he reached for her, sneaking a finger inside the elastic of her panties, touching her deep inside.

Her eyes closed as her hands stilled momentarily. The scrap of silk was forced aside as he cupped her with his hand, torturing her sweetly with his fingers. She moaned softly, fingers working at his button and zipper. She rested her hands on the edge of the desk, bowing backwards as his mouth closed over a silk-encased nipple.

"Dammit, Ell, I don't have a condom," he ground out, one hand bracing the middle of her back, the other still working its magic as her knees weakened.

"It's okay. You don't need one," she replied breathlessly. She worked against gravity and forced herself more upright so she could reach inside his trousers and shorts and take him in her hand. So hot, so smooth. His fingers stilled and she felt powerful, knowing her touch had made him forget everything but what her hand was doing. She shifted, perched on the edge of the desk, guided him forward. Devin ripped the scrap of fabric aside and she guided him inside her.

And oh, the feeling. Hot and hard and soft and utterly right. He slid deep, paused, and the connection between them rocked her to the core.

And then he was moving, and her head tipped back, reveling in the feeling of him inside her, touched to the soul by the depth of their union, surrendering to him in the only way she knew how. She heard his name on her lips, a thought given voice. She heard his murmured response and tightened her legs around his waist, linking her shoes behind his back as the sensations grew more demanding, threatening to take over everything. Her skin tingled as her muscles began to contract with urgency. She looked up at Devin. His eyes were focused on hers, so intense they were like blue fire burning into her soul. She bit down on her lip as his arm came around the middle of her back, holding her close as she came completely undone around him.

She was dimly aware of his forceful thrusts as her muscles liquefied. And then he too stilled and the only sound in the office was their harsh breathing, amplified in the passionate silence.

"Ella."

He held her close so that her cheek rested on his chest, and she felt the vibration of her name even as she heard it. He was still inside her and the feel of him there made her want to weep. It felt like it was exactly where he belonged. And for the first time ever, she questioned her decision to leave him all those years ago. He had been right at the cabin. She had walked out on their marriage. And yet to stay, she had been certain—was still certain, for that matter—that she would have ended up resenting him.

Oh God, it was so confusing. Wanting a man, loving a man and yet knowing you were absolutely wrong for each other.

And now he was part of her job. How on earth was she going to play the angle in the story now? Why would Dev take it upon himself to pay thousands of dollars for a neighbor's treatment? Why Betty? Every instinct she had told her there was more to the story.

Her heart was telling her it would be wrong to expose his secrets, whatever they might be. But she had always been loyal to the truth. There was no room for loyalty elsewhere. She couldn't do both.

"Let me up," she whispered, reality seeping in. How could she have let herself be swept away for a moment's passion— again? Her cheeks heated as she realized she was splayed across his desk in her underwear. She had been crazy, plain and simple. All it had taken was one touch from him and her body went up in flames, taking her perspective with it.

Dev removed his arm from around her back and straightened, pulling away. She flushed as he retrieved his shirt from the floor and shrugged it on, tucking everything away until he hardly looked rumpled.

She, on the other hand, had to adjust her underwear and pull up the left stocking that had rolled down as Dev had caressed her leg. She couldn't look him in the eyes as she tugged on her skirt and zipped it, picked up her jacket and put it on, buttoning the front and tugging it into place.

Her hairpins were scattered on the floor. Even if she could find all of them, without a mirror she had no hope of putting the twist back into her hair. She smoothed it with her hands as best she could and let the waves flow over her shoulders. And hoped his receptionist wouldn't remember her hairstyle from when she'd arrived.

Ella gathered up all the courage she had. Devin had the power to distract her from everything she'd ever wanted. She couldn't let that happen again. She went to her briefcase and pulled out a plain beige file.

"If you could explain this, that'd be great." She held out the papers and willed her hand not to shake. She had to get her story first. Work before pleasure. Devin was hiding far more than an anonymous donation, and she intended to get to the bottom of it.

Then he would see he had to sign the papers. He had to set her free. He had to. She couldn't move forward if their marriage still held her tied to the past.

Devin came forward slowly and took the papers from her hands. He flipped through the sheets, looking up sharply once. "You've read everything here?"

"This isn't just about Betty anymore. As you can see, there are significant gaps."

"Your source..."

She attempted a thin smile. "I'm sure you're aware that even giving this much information goes against confidentiality. My source took a huge risk getting me this much, and I'm not at liberty to reveal who they are. So now I'm asking you for the truth."

"I can find out."

"You won't find out from me." She held her ground on that one.

He sighed, dropping the sheaf of papers on his desk. "Why now? Oh, I suppose it's because now I have money. I'm worth something, right? It makes it easier to put the screws to me if I have something to lose."

Ella thought of their marriage, thought of the baby inside her, thought of the life she'd attempted to make for herself. He had no idea of the real stakes here. This wasn't about punishing him for being successful. At least not for her.

"What did you think? That I waited until you made your fortune and then stepped in to claim my portion?"

He raised his eyebrows. "The thought occurred."

Ella stepped back. She was happy he'd become a success. It was what she had wanted for him. For them even. A chance to move out of a ramshackle cabin and have a good life. But it was more complicated than simply being for the money.

"You really thought I was capable of that?"

"How was I to know, Ella?"

"Because you know me."

"No, I don't."

Ella's heart sank at those words. He didn't know her, did he? She hadn't let him see the woman she'd become. And she really didn't know him either. She swallowed thickly. The feeling flooding her earlier had been love. She was smart enough to know that. But love for the Devin she'd left behind. In so many ways the man sitting across from her was a stranger.

"So that's why you didn't sign them before I left?"

He looked up at her, his gaze dark and serious. "I called my lawyer when you were sleeping. He advised me not to sign anything. Both of us found it difficult to believe you didn't know about DMQ and my bank account."

That he thought so little of her hurt. Yes, she'd left him, but she wasn't back now as a gold digger and he should know it. "As much as it makes me either a rotten journalist or suffering from a gigantic lack of curiosity, no, Devin, I didn't know. I didn't have a clue about DMQ until I saw the company name listed in reference to Betty Tucker. I swear it on my mama's grave."

Devin sobered then. He knew as well as she that it was an oath she would not take lightly.

"May I have the divorce papers, please? I assume you brought them."

Relief rushed through Ella, almost heady in its arrival. She reached into her case and took out the other envelope, placing it before him on the desk.

He took the sheaf out of the envelope, turned the pages once more, while anxiety curled its way through her stomach. Just sign them, she thought. Sign them and let me get my story and that will be the end of it.

He reached for a pen, flipped to the last page. She held her breath and her gaze followed his hand as it hovered over the blank line.

The he put down the pen. He lifted the papers in front of her eyes, gripped the edge in his fingers and tore them down the middle.

"I don't want a divorce," he said plainly, putting the ruined contract on the desk where they'd just had sex.

And for the first time since taking the pregnancy test, Ella felt nauseous.

Ella had always wanted to stay at the Strater, but there had never been the money, not when her mother had been alive or even when she and Devin had been married. They'd spent their wedding night at the cabin instead of luxuriating in the thick sheets and ordering room service. Today she had defiantly booked a room. Because she could, and she wanted Devin to know he wasn't the only one who'd made good on youthful aspirations. And she'd also done it out of necessity—there was no sense flying back to Denver today. She'd have to change her ticket. There was the small matter of getting to the root of Betty's story as well as working out their personal issues. Devin had paid for Betty's treatment. But why? There was more to this than an insurance company's refusal to pay benefits. There was a human element she could not deny. And somehow her husband was right in the middle of it.

Maybe her boss wanted the bare facts, but for her that wasn't enough.

She sat on the edge of the plush bed, staring around the historic suite. How had she gotten herself into this mess? Why hadn't she listened to her lawyer's advice? It would have been a whole different matter investigating the story if she and Devin were not married. Talk about conflict of interest. She'd thought about asking to be taken off the story, but was afraid it would look grossly unprofessional. Plus she would have had to explain why it was a conflict of interest—that Devin was in fact her husband. The last thing she needed was to bring her messed-up personal life to work. So she'd kept her mouth shut.

Now she was in deeper than ever and feeling guilty to boot. How could she follow a career dream to Boston still married to Devin? How would she manage being a single mother? Despite it being completely unplanned, she already knew the thought of any other alternative was out of the question. This child would know his or her mother. The two problems combined to provide the biggest one of all. She'd grown up not knowing her dad. She couldn't in all conscience keep the secret from Devin, but how in the world could they possibly agree on how to co-parent?

She lay down on the covers, closing her eyes. Oh, that one got her every time. The guilt she felt now was nothing compared to what she'd feel later. He would have to know, but now was not the right time. The decisions about their marriage had to be about the two of them, not influenced by a baby. That was too much of a responsibility for a child to bear. She should know. It was unfair to put the success of a marriage on a baby's shoulders.

He had to see reason. Great sex was not enough to carry a

relationship. Opportunity and a fresh start were in Boston. And Devin's life was here, as it always had been. Their lives were too different. No matter what he said, he was married to DMQ now. She'd put this off for far too long. She would make the break, divorce or no divorce. Then she'd tell him about the baby once she was settled in Boston.

She kicked off her shoes and heard the muffled thump as they hit the floor. After he'd ripped up the divorce papers she'd felt light-headed and had sat, shocked that he'd do such a thing. He had been booked solid for meetings during the afternoon, and she hadn't been sure what to do next. Devin had been utterly in control of the situation, getting his way and making demands. The fact that he was so easily able to dismiss her after they'd made love stung. And there was the small matter of not getting what she'd come for.

She had to regroup. So she'd made her excuses and invited him for dinner at the hotel. Over dinner they could talk about Betty Tucker and DMQ, because she was sure that was where the true story lay. And then she would make him see reason. He would stay on his side of the table, and she'd stay on hers. If they could manage that, there would be a way out of this mess. The cost of the room would be worth it if she could come out of this in one piece.

Her eyelids grew heavy as she gave into the fatigue that seemed to plague her most afternoons. She'd have a little nap and then prepare for Devin's arrival.

And this time she would not let him distract her.

That thought was still floating in her mind when she opened her eyes three hours later. She checked her watch. Where had the time gone? She'd never napped so long in her life. As she went to the bathroom to splash her face with water, she ruefully admitted to herself that the combination of hormones, stress and sex had probably contributed to her need for rest. But now she was refreshed. And without a change of clothing. Before she met Devin at six, she needed something else to wear. The suit of this morning would never do.

She made her way along Main Avenue, window shopping. Some of the stores she remembered, others were new additions to the local retail scene. One boutique in particular looked promising and she went in. Thirty minutes later she came out with a bag containing a pretty, yet classy black dress that she could wear with her silver heels. No more stockings either. Practical, all-the-way-up pantyhose. In deference to the fall weather, she had bought a soft wrap for over her shoulders. Years ago such a shopping spree would have been impossible. She lifted her chin. That she was able to do so now was a testament to her own success. Devin wasn't the only one who'd made good. She'd supported herself quite well. She had to remember that.

One more stop produced a pair of plain cotton pajamas, jeans, a long sleeved T-shirt and an irresistible pair of funky sneakers that were white with multi-coloured polka dots. There was no reason she shouldn't opt for comfort when she was off the clock. Tomorrow, when she flew back to Denver, it would be nice to do it in jeans rather than a skirt and heels.

She checked her watch, her confidence restored. Devin was on her turf now. Ripping up the papers was perhaps a godsend. Now she'd focus on the story rather than being torn between the two objectives. When she got back to Denver, she'd make the move to file without his signature.

Devin slammed the door to his car and hit a button on his keychain activating the alarm. He smiled a little to himself as he

125

looked up at the historic hotel. The Strater. He knew exactly what game Ella was playing. He'd screwed up all her plans by ripping up the divorce papers. Now she was seeking to reestablish control by putting things on her turf—and in the Strater, no less. In some ways he liked the new Ella. She was predictable, but she was a worthy adversary. Tearing the decree hadn't been his plan, but in the moments after their lovemaking he'd realized a bold stroke was needed. The last time he'd simply not signed. This was definitely a better statement. He hadn't been able to fight for her last time. That wasn't the case now.

She'd called his office and left a message with her room number and time. Fine. He'd dance to her tune this much, let her think she was in control.

He knocked on her door and after a few seconds she answered, and the sight of her was like a punch to the solar plexus, the kind that took him utterly by surprise and stole all his breath. She'd changed into a new dress, something black and flowy, hinting at her curves and practically shouting class and femininity all at once. Her hair, which he'd enjoyed liberating from its severe pins this morning, hung loosely down her back, pulled back from the sides in a simple, almost invisible clip. Her color was back too. Her cheeks were pink, pinker by the moment as they stared at each other, and she seemed to glow at him.

He'd never stopped loving his wife. After that first night at the cabin, when he'd tucked her into bed, he'd suspected. He wanted to believe her when she said she had no ulterior motives about the divorce. She'd been after it for enough years it made sense, he supposed.

But how could he convince her to change her mind? Ella was stubborn. She'd hold on to a point even if she knew she was wrong, strictly on the basis of pride. That strength was something he was coming to love in the new Ella. Her stubbornness even helped feed the fire between them. He found himself looking forward to their verbal sparring. Almost as much as he looked forward to holding her in his arms.

He would get his way. He always did. He was used to looking at the big picture and being patient. But this time the goal was so close he could nearly taste it.

Or maybe that was the light, fresh scent of her perfume teasing his senses. He swallowed.

"Are you standing there all day or coming in?" She stood back, holding the door open.

"In," he replied, stepping inside the room. He looked around at the antique furniture, the unique style of historical blended with the opulent. Despite having lived around Durango all his life, he'd never been inside one of these rooms. It had been a particular dream of theirs to spend a night here and instead he'd invested in his own vacation properties and the Animas Resort.

But as Ella went to the dining table and lit a candle, his body experienced a familiar tensing. Perhaps tonight they'd have their night.

Chapter Eight

Ella lit the candles on the table, using the opportunity to present her back to Devin and catch her breath. Lord, he looked handsome. Sexy. Even a little...dangerous. It was the glint in his eye. The curve of his lips. It was also the powerful memory of making love with him in his office this morning. It was potent enough to make a woman stop and think.

But she had to keep her eye on the prize. Relax. Get him talking. She had to put their personal relationship to one side for the present. She needed to know why he'd paid for Betty's bills with no obvious benefit to himself. Her boss had sensed there was a story and she got the same feeling. Finding it meant she would be one step closer to a better job and a new life. Devin was a prominent businessman these days, and people loved reading about one of their own. The fact that Devin was persistently keeping it hidden had to mean it was significant. Why else wouldn't he just tell her?

The ability to focus on work was almost a relief, to be honest. She shook the match, extinguishing it, and exhaled. Putting off their other issues until another time lightened the weight on her shoulders. At least this interview was something she could control.

"I thought we could dine in," she said softly, pasting a smile to her face. Not too bright, not suggestive. Friendly. Trying to make him comfortable and ask the questions she needed to ask while sitting in a restaurant seemed counterproductive. She needed him to let his guard down. "That way we can talk without being overheard."

Devin came farther inside the room, slowly, taking his time as he went past a high table adorned with fresh flowers. She watched with fascination as he trailed his finger over the petal of a bronze chrysanthemum. A finger that had just this morning slid up the tender skin of her thigh...

"Just talk?" he asked finally, and she suddenly felt bereft of oxygen at the subtle taunting hidden in the words. She reminded herself to breathe. That she was sexually attracted to Dev was indisputable. She always had been, ever since puberty hit and she'd finally understood the fuss about the differences between boys and girls. Of course, in those days desire took the form of learning to kiss and holding hands while her heartbeat quickened. These days it was hotter, faster and more dangerous.

But it wasn't enough anymore. As she stared at him in his suit, she compared him to the jeans-and-boots man she'd encountered all those weeks ago. That man was comfortable in the battered pickup truck. The Devin she'd encountered this morning dressed in tailored suits and drove the SUV she'd seen parked in front of his offices. While the successful businessman before her still seemed capable of ringing her bell, she realized she did not know who he was any longer. He'd changed. He had a harder edge to him that made her uncomfortable. Despite his generosity towards Betty, there was a part of him that seemed willing to do whatever it took to get what he wanted. Tearing up the papers today was a prime example.

How far would he go once he found out about the baby? Her fingers lightly touched her still-flat stomach. Could he really be ruthless? If he knew about the baby, the divorce would be a non-issue. He'd been clear about wanting children from the beginning, when the time was right. If he found out she was carrying his child he'd never let her go. It wouldn't matter where she lived. She'd never be free to live her own life.

What had happened this morning had been borne out of lust and perhaps flavored with memories. But it hadn't been about Devin and Ella *now*.

So answering, "Yes, just talk," came easier than she would have expected. She gestured with a hand, desperately trying to erase her thoughts about their personal relationship and keep things business. "Please, sit down and have a look at the menu. You must be hungry."

He waited until she was seated at the small table before sitting himself, a courtesy she hadn't expected. The Devin she'd known had lacked polish, simply because he'd never been in a position to learn it. But he seemed to slide into those good manners now as easily as he'd slid onto his couch for the ball game at the cabin. Her brow wrinkled slightly as she picked up the menu. Which one was the real Devin? Perhaps after tonight she'd know. She'd know why a man with only a passing acquaintance with Betty Tucker as a boy became a man who helped with her household chores and went so far as to spend tens of thousands of dollars on her medical care. How far would he go for a child he loved? She had a suspicion she already knew the answer. To the ends of the earth.

"Do you want to share a starter?" he asked quietly. She lifted her eyes over the rim of the menu and met his gaze. Why, after all that had transpired between them lately, did he suddenly feel like a complete stranger? Like she was on some kind of a blind date?

"Perhaps the grilled shrimp?" She'd looked at the appetizer menu and other than a salad, the shrimp was all that appealed.

She'd never had that problem before. But as each day passed, she was realizing that pregnancy changed a lot of things—big and small. Appetite was the tip of the iceberg. And she had to eat. Another lightheaded spell and Dev would start noticing something was off.

"Sounds good. If you're ready, I can call down..."

Ella stood, amazed when Dev made the move to do so as well. "It's all right," she said, waving a hand. "I invited you here, remember? I can order for us. Just tell me what you want."

He did and she called in the order. But as she hung up the phone, she realized she should have preordered for them because now the minutes until their food came would tick away at a snail's pace.

"Would you like a drink?" She held up a bottle of chilled sparkling water. "Or I can order up something a little stronger if you'd like."

"The water is fine," he replied. He pushed back his chair and came forward, his shoes making no sound on the carpeted floor. Her hand wobbled as she poured the liquid into a glass and held it out. The fact that there was a four-poster bed in the room hadn't escaped her notice. But there would be no using it this evening. She was determined.

"Thank you." He took the glass, sipped, peered into her face. "What's got you so nervous, Ell? You're jumpier than a frog at courtin' time." He smiled at her, the dimple in his cheek threatening to pop. Like he knew exactly what was making her nervous.

She sipped and concentrated on making her face relax. "Nothing," she replied, raising an eyebrow. "I'm hungry though. I didn't have much lunch."

It was the wrong thing to say. He frowned, coming even closer so that she couldn't escape the heady scent of his aftershave. "And you were pale this morning. Are you sure you're feeling all right?"

"I feel fine," she replied, taking a deeper drink and bravely meeting his eyes. She had dutifully bought a turkey sandwich and carton of milk after leaving his office, knowing the queasiness that had recently appeared only got worse on an empty stomach. But that was long gone. She looked up into his eyes, unable to remain untouched by his concern. "I truly just need something to eat, and I'll be right as rain," she replied.

She needed to deflect the conversation from herself before Dev started asking more questions. "So until our food comes, why don't you tell me why you paid Betty Tucker's medical bills?"

Devin considered as he sipped the deplorable sparkling water. God, he hated this stuff. Bubbles were meant to have some flavor. Champagne would have been a better choice in his opinion. He wondered if she'd be surprised to learn he'd developed a taste for it.

Ella seemed determined to not talk about herself. She was wasting no time in getting to the heart of the matter. This was why she'd come to Durango. It said something that the story meant more to her than their divorce. And Ella was clearly in her get-the-story mode. She needn't be. He was only putting her through the paces because he wanted to make her work for it. Ever since she'd reappeared he'd known this moment was coming. Tearing up the papers meant the time was coming soon. And in some ways he wanted her to finally know the truth.

But not this way. When he'd ripped up the papers today, he'd hoped her invitation was a good sign. After they'd made love again he'd said it straight out—he didn't want a divorce.

And she'd invited him to dinner in her hotel room. What was he supposed to think?

Clearly, the wrong thing. Because she wanted the truth, but for her story, not for herself or for their relationship. He was disappointed in her. And yet proud of her strength and focus.

"I paid Betty's bills because she needed the treatment and there was no other way she was going to get it."

The room seemed very small to him just now. The options were to stand, to sit at the dining table or sit on the bed. While his body responded to the last thought, he knew this wasn't the time to answer the call of his libido. He fought against the confinement by releasing the button on his suit jacket.

"But why Betty?" Ella looked up at him over the rim of her glass. "There must be thousands of people like her. Ill and with no health benefits."

"But Betty is here, and she's one of us," he replied. He went to the table and refilled his glass, drinking the despicable water just to keep his hands busy. She wasn't asking the right questions, and that annoyed him. This wasn't about Betty at all. He pretended to sip the liquid as he stared at her. She was still the most beautiful woman he'd ever known. Why couldn't she see that he would never have given her up unless he'd had no choice?

"Does it really matter? She needed the help and I gave it."

"If I've learned anything, it's that people *always* have a motive. Altruism is never random. So why don't you tell me about the rest? Besides the really big check you wrote?"

She stepped forward now, and he knew her senses had sharpened. She thought she was getting to the meat of the story, when it really went so much deeper than this.

"What rest?"

"She told me you delivered groceries, painted her porch, hired her a cleaning lady... All sorts of things. Why would you do that? You didn't answer me the last time. I believe you tried to distract me instead."

Devin looked away. Betty had been kind to him once. More than kind. He wanted Ella to know the truth, but he didn't want to read about it in the press. He'd never wanted to capitalize on his misfortune. So before they went any further, he needed to know her intentions.

"What kind of story do you want to write, Ella?" He put down the glass. "What do you want with me? Do you want to expose the HMO? Do you want a human interest piece on me? Rags-to-riches story, poor boy who grows up to be a great philanthropist? Because that's not me. That's not who I am."

He went to her and gripped her upper arms. "Think carefully before you answer."

She bit down on her lip and his eyes followed the motion, seeing her even, white teeth worry at the soft, pink flesh.

"Can't I do both?"

"You know you can't."

A knock at the door interrupted and he dropped his hands, stepping back. The rest of the evening depended on her answer. Her motives mattered.

"That will be room service." She tucked a tiny piece of hair behind her ear and straightened her shoulders. He watched her walk to the door, all heels and shapely calves and appetizing curves. The doubt and confusion he'd seen in her eyes gave him hope. This wasn't easy for her. Perhaps the soft, caring girl he'd fallen in love with was still there, inside. Had his part in their separation helped make her jaded? He wondered if he'd been able to fight for her all those years ago if it would have made any difference.

The meal was placed before them: sizzling shrimp, pepper steak, another bottle of sparkling water. Devin watched Ella as it was laid out on the table. She didn't drink when working, he realized. Tonight, when a bottle from the restaurant's extensive list would have been a perfect pairing, she was sticking to fancy water. He couldn't help but respect it the smallest bit. It spoke to a professionalism he admired. In his business, he'd seen too many deals signed over a few drinks fall apart later.

But Ella wasn't strictly business. She was still his wife. Even though the new Ella was different from the girl he'd married, his respect for her grew another notch. Whatever she did, she did with commitment. He couldn't help but admire that quality, even if her professional attention was working against him.

Ella resumed her seat at the table and he followed as the wait staff faded away and out the door. Devin lifted his glass. "To a room at the Strater. We only had to wait a decade or so."

Her cheeks colored, the pink flush very becoming next to her golden hair and the black fabric of her dress. "Devin," she warned.

But he smiled in return, wanting to tease out all the good parts of Ella he'd glimpsed. They'd had hopes and dreams. And despite it being a backwards route, they were here nonetheless and in one of the finest rooms at that. "A simple observation, Ella, that's all. Did you think I'd forgotten?"

And he held his glass out, waiting for her to accept the toast.

Ella lifted her glass and touched the rim to his. She could feel the blush in her cheeks, put there not only by Devin's words but by his soft smile. Something had shifted in the last few minutes, though she didn't know just what. But the edge, the protective layer she'd sensed around him was suddenly gone. She took a sip of water, grateful he hadn't mentioned the lack of alcohol. Water, milk and apple juice seemed to be the big three for her now.

"Try the shrimp," he suggested.

She dipped one of the shrimps in the sauce and nibbled, the flavor exploding on her tongue. Lordy, she was famished. And the steak smelled heavenly. There was something about red meat lately that was so appetizing. Hamburgers, steak, roast beef sandwiches. Normally she was a chicken or fish girl. But tonight when Devin had told her his order, it had sounded so good she'd ordered the same for herself.

"It's delicious. Try one."

For a few minutes, they enjoyed their meal, but after the first sampling bites were over with, they settled into conversation.

"You never did answer my question," Dev prodded, cutting into his steak. "About the story. That is why I'm here, isn't it?"

The alternative was that he was here about the divorce, and Ella didn't want to think about that just yet. With Dev, the topic of the divorce just spun them in circles and it made her dizzy. "Yes, that's why you're here. And to answer your question, the article is about Betty. I already hit the HMO in my first installment. And yes, my assignment was to get to the bottom of why you would pay for her treatment." She considered for a moment and decided the truth was the best approach at this point. For some reason she felt she owed him the truth, at least about this. "My boss wants to know why a successful Colorado entrepreneur would do such a thing. And why he'd keep quiet about it."

Devin laid his knife along the rim of his plate. "And what do you want, Ella?"

"Professionally, I want to paint a picture of an ordinary,

brave, compassionate woman caught in a horrible set of circumstances."

"And personally?"

"On a personal level, I want to know why Dev McQuade, successful Colorado entrepreneur would be her knight in shining armor, paying out of his pocket and expecting nothing in return." He started to open his mouth but she continued, meeting his gaze with her own, needing him to understand. She didn't want him to walk away thinking she was hard and uncaring, inconsiderate of people's privacy. "What I want to know and what I will write about are two very different things. I want to write about Betty. Not for my own gain. But to put a human face on her situation. To make people care. The way you seem to care."

Nerves seemed to bubble and froth in her tummy as she finished. The article she'd just described was not the same article she'd been assigned, and yet she'd meant what she said. It was like Devin was testing her and she had no idea if she'd passed. Nor did she quite understand why it mattered so much for Dev to approve. She could have gone back to Betty for the information. She could have avoided Dev altogether if she'd wanted.

Sitting across from him now, she realized she'd wanted to hear it from him. Instinct told her there was a bigger story here than she could imagine. More than that, her life was changing. And although she could hardly admit it to herself, she had wanted to see him one more time. When she'd found out about DMQ, she had needed to see him for what he'd become. Not as the boy she'd left behind. But the man he'd grown into. To somehow reconcile the two sides into one person. She couldn't shake the idea that somehow Betty Tucker played a part in it.

"I have no desire to expose you in print, Dev. I just know

there is something more. A bigger explanation." She was surprised to feel her lip quiver with emotion. "We never used to have secrets, you and me, and I can't help but feel that this is a part of your life I didn't share. I know it's not fair of me to ask. But I want to know for me. Not for selling copies or job promotions. For me."

Silence hummed for a few moments, until Dev replied quietly, "What do you want to know?"

Ella swallowed the bite of steak she'd been chewing. "I left twelve years ago. DMQ was registered as a company eight years ago. But there are four years missing. Four years that are a big blank. That's what I want to know about. What happened in that time? What happened to you, Dev? What led up to DMQ being formed? And how does Betty fit into it? Because I'm fairly certain she does somehow."

"You're very astute."

"It's my job."

"And you're good at your job, aren't you?"

"Better than I get credit for." She smiled then, feeling a bit of the old confidence come back.

He studied her for a few moments. "And yet you didn't know about DMQ until recently. Doesn't it seem strange to you? It's not like it was hidden information."

"I never went looking." She stared at her plate now, afraid of what Devin would see in her eyes. The truth. It wasn't for lack of research skills or even curiosity. It was far more personal.

"You never once Googled me, researched Durango or the Gulch."

Her cheeks heated and it became an effort to swallow even the smooth, sweet chutney that came with the steak. "No."

He sat back in his chair, disbelieving. "Was leaving me that easy? Just turn your back and walk away, never looking over your shoulder?"

"No." She braved a look up then, knowing she couldn't lie anymore. Not to him, not to herself. "Leaving you was the hardest thing I've ever done. And the only way I could do it was to cut all ties. My heart couldn't take checking up on you, clinging to things you'd done, what you might look like. I loved you too much and it would have been torture."

His lips fell open then and she pushed the meal away, suddenly not hungry anymore. "How's that for honesty?"

Devin ran a hand over his face, his eyes deep with surprise and she would swear with regret. "If it hurt so much, why do it?"

The words were there, waiting, but she thought again of the baby inside her, thought of the child she'd been and the mistakes she'd made, and her throat tightened. She shook her head, unable to say anything.

Devin too pushed away his half-eaten dinner.

Finally, Ella gathered the will to say something. "In many ways, Dev, I waited. I waited for you to come find me. To try to convince me. To..." For some reason emotion swamped her, drawing her back to those days when she'd lived in a dormitory, only change in her pocket and a huge student loan, waiting for Devin to come for her. Her voice broke as she finally admitted the truth. "I wanted you to fight for me. I wanted to know I was worth fighting for."

"You tested me."

"I didn't know that was what I had done until I was older, smarter. At the time I was only full of myself and my dreams and seeing all the other girls around me having fun. I was different from them. I was married already and I felt like I'd missed out on something. I saw them with their clothes and boyfriends and fun and all I could see was my mother waiting tables after my dad walked out. She never gave up waiting for him to come back. She looked for him in every boyfriend she had after he left her. That's what scared me. That I'd be caught and be too much like my mother to have my own life."

She sniffled, lifted her napkin and dabbed her nose. "It wasn't until later as I grew up that I could truly see. I did test you. I wanted you to fight for me the way my dad never did. I wanted the proof that I meant everything to you. The proof never came so I...I just had to put you out of my mind. My lack of curiosity was really just self-preservation."

"Ella..." Dev got out of his chair and came to her side, squatting beside her chair and taking her hand. She looked down into his eyes, feeling her heart being ripped to shreds as his thumb moved over her wrist and the lips that so often smiled in that devilish way were stone cold sober.

"You broke my heart when you left."

"So why didn't you come after me?"

"Would I have had the power to change your mind?"

She sighed, feeling like crying but trying not to. "I don't know. Maybe." She thought about the nights in her dorm room, all alone, feeling like she was unsophisticated and socially inept. She imagined what it would have been like if Devin, her handsome, sexy husband, had knocked on her door, telling her it was all right, encouraging her on. She blinked rapidly. "Yes," she admitted. "You probably could have changed my mind."

Devin rose, went to the bed, sat on the edge and put his head in his hands.

"It's too late for regrets. Please, just let it go."

He lifted his head, but what Ella hadn't expected to see was the abject torture in his eyes, the way his lips seemed to curve downwards in some sort of mental pain. He looked so incredibly unhappy Ella did not know what to say.

But Dev spoke instead.

"You ask why I didn't go after you. The truth is I couldn't."

"What do you mean, couldn't? And getting back on track for a moment, how does any of this tie into you feeling so obligated to Betty? Because it does, doesn't it? I can feel it. What is it you're not telling me?"

Resting his hands on his knees, she saw Devin take a breath while she held hers. The air in the room shimmered, as if waiting on the cusp of something.

His gaze locked with hers.

"I couldn't come after you because I was where Betty is. I had cancer."

Chapter Nine

"Cancer?" Ella stiffened, shock rippling through her body. Cancer? But they'd been married in August. She'd gone to school at the first of September. A few months later they were over. It seemed impossible. He'd been healthy, strong and tanned when she left. The very idea struck fear into her heart, leaving her cold. *Cancer.* Perhaps the most hated word in the English language. It was utterly wrong to pair it with *Devin.*

"Yes, cancer. A brain tumor."

She stared at him, looking at his thick, dark hair, his golden skin, his clear, beautiful blue eyes. Instantly a vision passed through her brain, of Devin, pale, bald, in a hospital bed, tubes and monitors attached to his frail body. The picture seemed to take the life right out of her, sucking it away until she felt like an empty vessel. She couldn't reconcile the two images. The young man he'd been then, the man before her now—he was so vital, so *alive.*

"A...A..."

She stammered as her lips refused to form the words. The floor felt odd beneath her feet. Devin had had cancer. And she'd been stuck in a dorm waiting for him to rescue her. Angry that he didn't at least try. Oh God, if she'd only known, she'd have...

She'd have what? Gone back? Forgotten about the mistake they'd made?

But her heart protested. She would have simply been there to help him. To sit by his side and hold his hand, if nothing else. She squeezed her eyes shut. How could she have comforted him, wondering if he was going to die? Even now, when he was healthy and strong before her, the very idea drained the energy from her body.

"A brain tumor. You can say it, Ella. I've been cancer free since Christmas that year."

Ella felt the floor moving, strangely getting closer as the room began to darken around the edges. She reached out for the side table but missed the edge as she crumpled out of her chair.

"Ell? Oh God, Ell, I never thought you'd faint." The words seemed to come from far away.

She was dimly aware of being held in his arms as he knelt on the floor. How many seconds had elapsed? Surely not many. She vaguely remembered him saying the words "cancer free" before things started spinning.

Her Dev. So very ill, and she'd known nothing about it. She'd taken his silence for anger—or worse, apathy. Instead he'd been sick, and she felt guilty for even thinking those awful things about him back then.

His arms tightened around her as he held her against his thighs. She pushed up, but that meant her hands were on his chest. His very alive, strong, warm chest. Funny how suddenly she appreciated that fact.

"A brain tumor," she repeated, knowing she sounded silly but unable to refrain. She lifted her hand and let her fingers touch the rich softness of his hair. She couldn't imagine him having his head shaved, and she traced his hairline down his temple to his ear. Did he have scars on his scalp? He must.

143

How long had he been in hospital? So many questions.

She closed her eyes as the guilt poured in. Had he read her "Dear Devin" letter while lying in a hospital bed? No wonder he had hated her. The simmering anger she'd felt bubbling beneath his charm that first weekend at the cabin made more sense now.

She opened her eyes and saw his brilliant blue ones watching her patiently. The veneer she'd seen in his gaze was gone, replaced by honesty. This was what he'd been hiding then. So many times she'd felt like he was the same Devin and yet different, like he was holding something back, more of a stranger. This was what he'd been holding on to, protecting.

She'd said goodbye to their marriage, to him, her best friend...and in return he'd fought his cancer all alone. How could she have been so self-absorbed? And why hadn't he trusted her with it? He had to know she would have been there for him. Or had he thought so little of her that he had written her off as quickly as she had him?

"So now you know," he said gently, and suddenly he was the boy she'd left behind again. The one who had always stood beside her as they'd grown, who'd refused to tease her like the other kids, who had taken her side more times than she could count. The boy who had taken her fishing and laughed at her when she refused to clean her own catch. It no longer mattered about his wealth, the cabin, wrong impressions. It all faded away until she saw the man she'd always known. Strong and loving.

And they had made a baby together.

Ella felt the magnitude of that fact envelop her soul. This pregnancy had the ability to nearly paralyze her with fear. Everything would change. She'd always been afraid of what having a child would mean to her life. But as she looked up into

Devin's face, she realized this baby, their baby, would be half of him.

Half of him, half of her. It was profound. Would he or she have blue eyes or brown? Dark hair or light? Be right handed or left? So many questions, so many possibilities...

She leaned forward, pressing a kiss to Devin's cheek as she put her arms around his neck. He pulled her close until she was snuggled in on his lap. He wasn't pushing her away. And this wasn't about sex. At the cabin and yes, even this morning, it had felt like it was about their physical relationship and getting each other out of their systems—hot and fast and thorough.

One word—cancer—had changed all of that. Having some of the pieces come together had resurrected the bond they'd shared since they had been children.

"I have so many questions," she whispered in his ear. "And yet, the one thing that I can't stop thinking is that I should have been here."

"Yes, you should have."

The quietly spoken words stung, and a tiny bit of anger sparked. Maybe she should have, but if he didn't tell her, how could she have known? Surely the blame wasn't all hers.

"How did... When did you find out? Why didn't you send for me? I would have come, I swear it." She kept her voice even, not wanting to pick a fight but needing to know anyway.

Devin sighed, ran his hand down her arm. "Would you, Ella? Are you sure you wouldn't have run farther away? I didn't know what to do. I had been feeling off all fall. When I found out, I knew I couldn't tell you over the phone. I thought it could wait until Thanksgiving when you came home. But before that your letter came. How could I go to you then? I didn't want you here out of obligation when your letter explained your feelings so clearly."

Her cheeks reddened because everything he was saying was true. She wanted to stir up some self-righteous defiance but she couldn't because it made sense. He'd wanted to tell her in person, not give such news over the phone or in a letter. And what had she done? Written a letter, ending their marriage. She'd had her reasons, but right now she felt like the largest coward on the planet.

Just like she was a coward for keeping the baby from him. She lowered her lashes so he wouldn't see the shame in her eyes. She would tell him. Not at this moment—there were too many other questions right now. But before she went back to Denver. Right now what he deserved was an apology for how she'd gone about things from the beginning.

"I didn't know what to do. I was scared and..." She took a breath. "And I was wrong. I know that now. I can say I was young and afraid but those are just excuses. I should have come home and told you how I was feeling, and instead I panicked."

"Would you have felt differently if you'd known I was sick? And how could I know if you were staying out of pity or love? I wanted to fight for you and I didn't have the energy. Why else did you think I didn't sign the papers when they first arrived? I wanted to be strong enough to fight. I was buying time."

"I was waiting for you to come for me, and you never did. I thought you didn't care—"

"Didn't care?" Devin pushed her away from him gently so he could look at her square in the face. "God, woman. I loved you with everything I was. I loved you, and I wanted to go after you. But the headaches got worse...nearly every morning, and one day I was at the drugstore for something to help and I collapsed and had a seizure."

A dark shadow seemed to pass over his eyes. "Betty was working that day and was the one who called 911."

Tears pricked behind Ella's eyelids. She was aware that they were still crouched on the floor and she offered a shaky smile. "I'm going to break your legs if you keep this up. Let's go sit."

She crawled off his lap, instantly feeling the lack of his warm body surrounding her. Her feet were steady now that the initial shock was over, and she held out her hand to him. Dev stood and they went to the bed. Devin sat, leaning back against the headboard and extending his legs, crossing his ankles. She watched him for a few moments, understanding how Betty fit into things now, knowing she had a story to write and feeling she had no right to tell it. She was good at not getting personally involved—she'd made a career of it. But this was beyond empathy, and she was sure being objective was impossible.

"Dev, I..." Ella stared at the plump mattress, wanting to go to him. Her head was shouting at her that the dining table would be a better, more neutral location. She hesitated, looked from the table and chairs back to Devin again.

He smiled his slow, slightly crooked smile. "I won't bite, sweetheart." His eyes shone at her, a little mischievous but utterly sincere. It was a combination Ella could not defend herself against. "Come sit with me, and I'll tell you everything."

She hesitated at the side of the bed, and then he patted the coverlet with his hand in invitation. Ella sat beside him, tucking her legs to the side on the mattress, resting her weight on her hand. She met his gaze. "Tell me everything. Make me understand."

For several seconds his gaze held her prisoner. "I'm not sure you will. I was angry for a long time."

"Are you still angry?"

Finally he broke eye contact, turning his head away. "Sometimes."

Apology had never come easily to Ella. It had always made her feel weak. It was confessing you'd made a mistake, made a wrong decision, and she hated that feeling. But today she knew she owed Devin an apology. Should they have stayed married? She only knew she'd done what she thought was right at the time. But how she'd done it was wrong. She'd realized it the first weekend they'd spent together. To argue the point now would only be false pride and needing to be right. If nothing else, she got the feeling that tonight was a time for unvarnished truth.

"I'm sorry, Dev. I'm sorry I left our marriage through a letter. If I was old enough to say 'I do' I should have been mature enough to face you when I thought we'd made a mistake. It was the wrong way to go about it. Things should have been said."

The silence spun out while Ella's stomach twisted with nerves. She and Devin had shared their innermost secrets growing up. But when it truly mattered—when it was their relationship at stake—neither of them had found the words. Maybe that was why they'd never been able to completely let go. It had nothing to do with legal papers and starting over. It had to do with finishing things first.

Now it would never be truly finished, she realized. They'd be forever joined by their child. The shaft of panic was immediately followed by a warmth she didn't quite understand.

"Before I explain any of this, I want your word it won't appear in print."

Ella hesitated, saw his jaw tighten as she said nothing for several seconds. She knew what her assignment had been. And she knew the story would make good copy. But she also knew this wasn't an interview. This was Devin, confiding in her. "I promise."

He seemed to accept her oath. "When I was first diagnosed, I was sure it was a mistake," Devin began softly, still not looking at her. "My mother and father were there for the surgery. They knew about the letter you'd sent and I made them promise they wouldn't contact you." He looked at her then, raised an eyebrow the slightest bit while a sad smile played on his lips. "Parents tend to take those things seriously when they think their child might be dying."

Ella remembered the one time in mid-November she'd tried calling the cabin, but there had been no answer. She'd wondered where Devin could be so late at night. She'd taken it as a sign their marriage was truly over and that he was already moving on—out for a night on the town. Now she realized he'd likely been in the hospital. Had he been in pain? Had he felt alone or had he been surrounded by those who loved him?

"They did my surgery right away. I was lucky. The tumor was removable and the after-effects were as good as we could have hoped for. But it was malignant and so once I was recovered enough, I had to have radiation." He smiled a little, adding a humorless laugh. "They'd already shaved my head. At least I didn't have to worry about my hair falling out, right? Although radiation is horribly hard on the skin."

The matter-of-fact words were sprinkled with cynicism. Ella didn't even realize she was crying until he finished speaking. Her cheeks felt wet and Devin sat up a bit, reached out and wiped away the moisture with his thumbs. "Don't cry. It doesn't matter now. Treatment was successful, obviously. And if it hadn't happened, maybe I'd never have built DMQ. All it cost me was my marriage."

The words were said with such bitterness that Ella had to turn away. She'd been afraid, sure. But it must have been so much worse for him. She should have been there. She should have come home to talk about it. At least then she would have known, and could have helped. The ache inside flashed once more with a little anger of her own. All he would have had to do was pick up the phone, drop her a note, send her an email. Yes, she'd been wrong. But so had he. He couldn't blame her for not being there when she'd had no idea of the situation.

"I made a mistake," she replied, wiping her fingers over her cheeks to get rid of the last dregs of her crying. "But so did you. You could have let me know. You could have let your mother call me and I would have come. For God's sake, I didn't hate you."

"You turned your back on our marriage."

"I was afraid. And that didn't mean I wouldn't have been there for you. I never stopped caring or..."

He leaned forward, slid a hand around her back and pulled her closer along the soft mattress, so that their chests nearly met. The candles on the table still flickered, casting shadows through the room now that evening was approaching.

"Or what, Ell?"

But she couldn't say it. Couldn't admit that she never stopped loving him. It put everything too much in the present, far too close.

"Or nothing," she murmured, looking down at the white bedspread. "I just wish you'd told me. It's a heck of a secret to keep. When I think of you, so ill, it's like someone's ripped a hole in my stomach, leaving this empty place behind. How did you ever convince your parents to promise?"

"They were so angry with you for leaving in the first place, it wasn't hard. All I had to do was show them your letter. Then I
150

made them swear on a Bible."

Ella's face flamed. The letter she'd written to Dev, pouring out her insecurities, covering them up with protests that they'd made a horrible mistake and she didn't want to be married to him anymore. That foolish, foolish letter. It was no wonder she had never heard from Mr. and Mrs. McQuade. That had hurt too, giving up the couple that had been the closest thing to two parents she'd ever known. The best example she'd had of how a marriage and family were supposed to work.

"How can you blame me for not being there when you wouldn't even tell me the truth? Did you hate me that much?"

Dev ran his hand through his hair, sighing, feeling on edge for the umpteenth time today. God Almighty, it had taken everything he had not to beg her to come back. But if he had, he would have always wondered why she'd done it. Would it have been out of love or sympathy? And he hadn't known what the prognosis would be. He'd wanted to protect her from the ugliness of hospitals and continuous treatments. Hell, maybe he should have set her free when she sent the divorce papers each time. But the truth was he'd wanted, needed, her to come to him and ask face-to-face.

"That was why I didn't come after you. I was too sick, too weak to fight—I was fighting for my life instead. I was not the man you'd married."

"And so that's why you stepped in and helped Betty."

"Yes. She helped me that day in the drugstore and she helped me in the days after. She brought me pie she'd made and books from the library She visited me in the hospital and held the cup and straw for me when I was too weak to do it for myself. She became like, I don't know, like a favorite aunt. She cared, and now I have my chance to finally repay that favor. I know what it is like to be afraid you are dying and then be burdened with the knowledge that you can't pay for any of it. If I can spare her that concern, I'm happy to do it.

"You didn't have any insurance either."

He shook his head, remembering getting the diagnosis and wondering where the money was going to come from. Wondering if he'd die before he could get proper treatment. "Not for that. You know my parents. Hell, we both grew up on the edges of poor. Whatever we had was the bare minimum."

It was true. The main difference in their families wasn't annual income. Instead it was the love they all seemed to share and a sense of family that she and her mother had never quite accomplished, it being just the two of them scraping by. Ella had never felt unequal next to Devin in her thrift store jeans and cheap T-shirts. Other girls were concerned with labels and having the latest "in" thing, but not Ella. There hadn't been money for that. Her mother had worked two jobs just to keep a roof over their heads. Devin had slightly better clothes, but there was no money for flash. He'd never judged her for it, and to her, he'd been the most gorgeous boy in school.

He still was, she admitted to herself. The best-looking man she'd ever known. One with the power to reach inside her and turn everything upside down.

"So how did you pay for it?" She leaned forward a tiny bit, reveling in the warmth radiating from his body, luring her in, cozy in its security. If she wasn't careful, she'd end up snuggled in his arms as they talked. And that would be dangerous indeed.

"I had to take all the money I'd saved—every penny—to pay the bills. My parents remortgaged their home, and even then it took a few years before it was paid for. How could I go to you then? I'd been saving since I was fifteen for the future. And every dime we'd put away towards our plans was gone. I was penniless, sick..."

He stopped as if he were suddenly choking on words. He released his hands and her body felt cold without the warmth of his nearness seeping through her dress. What could be worse than losing your wife and finding out you had a brain tumor? What else was he keeping from her?

They'd come this far. Sitting in a hotel room, on top of the covers, not beneath them. Being as honest as she could ever remembering being in her life. Nothing she'd rehearsed in her head this afternoon had prepared her for this. A simple reason behind Betty Tucker's bills had become a full-fledged post-mortem of their marriage.

He cleared his throat. "I was penniless, sick, afraid of dying. And I was afraid for you to see any of it."

"So you took my choice away." She pushed away and got up off the bed, feeling stronger than she had all day. Yes, she'd written that stupid letter. But he'd gotten all macho and manly and had cut her out. "And then you made me pay for it every year by your silence. Not caring and not setting me free either."

"I never said I didn't care." He slid off the bed as well and faced her. "You were the one who left me."

"I was scared, you idiot!" The outburst rang through the room. "You were always there to make things better, you know? And suddenly you weren't. And going home meant giving up. Leaving you meant finding the strength to stand on my own two feet."

The earlier softness in his eyes hardened, cooled. "I'm sorry I held you back so very much. Now you've got your story. Do what you will." He held up a hand, clearly dismissive and she chafed against the command. She'd do as she damn well pleased.

"Look, Devin. I'll buy that you didn't want to put me

through the cancer or whatever. But once you were well...you could have explained. I took your silence for assent. What was I supposed to think?"

"I was angry, Ella. So angry. At you, at life... The more time went on, the longer it went and still you didn't come, I refused to sign the papers each and every time you sent them. I hated you for leaving and for not coming back to end things the right way."

"I want to be able to blame you for that, and I can't," she admitted. If nothing else, seeing Dev again had made her grow up a little bit more. She'd pretended he didn't exist for too long. "We were both so stubborn. But I was too afraid to see you, to talk to you."

"Why?"

He raised his eyebrows as he asked the question, his gaze probing hers.

"Because I was afraid of my own weakness, Devin." Even now, standing this close to him, knowing what she did, she wanted him. Even as she fought to be heard, understood, she wanted to touch him, taste him. Even more than before, knowing what he'd been through. Now she longed to touch, to marvel at every square inch of his body. Oh, it was downright foolish, but she'd never had another lover. She'd never wanted one. In her heart she'd known no one would measure up to Dev.

"I was afraid that what would happen was exactly what *did* happen." She let a shy smile creep up her lips. "We ended up in bed."

But instead of the teasing grin she expected, he scowled, turning his head away.

"There's another reason why I didn't come after you," he muttered darkly. She stared at the stubborn jut of his chin, wondering what else she could have possibly done wrong all those years ago. Hadn't she been punished enough?

Her temper started to get the better of her and she lifted her chin. "Please," she said coldly, "tell me what else I did wrong. We might as well catalogue them all now and get it over with."

He turned back to her, his blue eyes blazing icily with resentment.

"Oh, it's not you." The words were almost a snarl, and he took a deep breath. The exhale came on a shudder that told her exactly how upset he was.

"How could I have asked you to come back, when I knew the treatment I'd had probably made me unable to give you the children we wanted?"

Chapter Ten

Ella's hands immediately went to her stomach, almost as a confirmation of the life that was growing within her. There wasn't even a telltale bump beneath her fingers, or movement of any sort. But it was there, growing, changing. Dev's child that he was afraid he could never have.

"But today...and the condom," Ella said, confused.

"It was never a definite diagnosis," he replied, the edges of his words sharp as glass.

Ella thought back to the night they'd shared. "And at the cabin..."

"I forgot. It's not right, but then today when you said it wasn't necessary, I figured you were on the pill or something anyway." He looked away, went back to the dining table and picked up his water glass, taking a sip of the water while Ella stared after him. At this moment he was so changed from the carefree, contented boy she'd known. They'd whispered plans in the dark, not just about what they would do but dreams of having their own family. A family with a mother and a father, one where the children were wanted and nurtured and could witness what a real, healthy relationship was like. A family like she'd never had. One he'd understood she always wanted. Now they were reduced to talking about birth control and mistakes.

Her hands still cradled her stomach, protecting. She and

Dev didn't have that kind of relationship any longer. Since seeing him they'd been on opposite sides time and again. And yet, how could she keep the baby a secret? How could she let him go on believing that he couldn't be a father, when she knew he already was to a bundle of cells they'd made together?

"Devin," she began, unsure of what to say. This was no longer about the story. She wouldn't turn in the article she was assigned. Any doubts she had on that score had fled. She couldn't—wouldn't—exploit him that way. "Devin, did the doctors specifically say you couldn't have children?"

He put the glass down on the table and she could tell by the stubborn set of his jaw that he was beginning to isolate himself. After all that had come out tonight, it was the last thing she wanted. Things were *finally* starting to make sense. His illness had changed everything for him then and it was changing everything for her now. Her old judgments no longer held.

"They said the treatments could affect my fertility and that I could have problems fathering a child, if at all."

"And so you gave up on us? Is this the real reason?" She took a step forward, her heart clubbing. She needed to hear his answer, craved it.

"You already had said you wanted a divorce. What did I have that could bring you back? My savings were gone, I wasn't sure if the cancer would return and the family we wanted was a pipe dream."

"But you never signed the papers..." She led him along with the question.

"As I said before, I wanted you to look me in the eye and ask. I didn't want it to be easy for you. It sure as hell wasn't easy for me."

His brow wrinkled a bit, as if he were trying to puzzle out

where she was going. Ella felt a sting behind her eyes as she took one more step, trying hard not to hope.

"And today when you ripped the papers?"

Finally, he made a move, taking a step across the carpeted floor to meet her. She watched him swallow, his Adam's apple bobbing and his chest falling slightly as he exhaled. He lifted his hand, grazed her cheek with his thumb. "I can't seem to stay away from you, Ell. I'm with you and I want to touch you. I'd rather argue with you than not talk at all. And I'd rather make love than argue. I agreed to come tonight because I thought you deserved to know the truth. I don't want a divorce. But you need to know that if we try to work this out, we might never have a family."

Ella's nerve endings were working overtime, in tune to the sound of his voice and the light touch upon her cheek. Stay married? That was what he wanted? Impossible. Their lives weren't even in the same city, and soon they would not even be in the same state. And yet a part of her thrilled to hear him say it. Her heart hummed with the possibility of being with him, pulsed with the knowledge that he wanted to be with her.

"Did I say I wanted to try to work things out?"

He shook his head, his gaze holding hers captive. "No. But if cancer taught me anything, it's how to hope."

She was defenseless against that argument. So many things were getting jumbled up. Her job, their relationship, their baby. A triangle of confusion and she wasn't sure they could reconcile any of them.

"I came here to find a story."

"And did you?"

She thought of Betty, and Dev, and the baby. "Not the one I thought. I won't use your disease to further my career." She looked into his piercing blue eyes. "I'll find another way."
158

His body was so close she knew one small move and she would be in his arms. But not yet. If she were going to do this—and she had to, or else she'd be awake all night—she had to keep her head straight. She couldn't do that while she was in his arms. His gaze dropped to her lips and she took a step backward.

"What story did you find, Ell?"

His voice was silky-smooth, seductive, and it nearly made her body weep with want. Suddenly the knowledge that she was carrying his child was unbearably sexy—a connection tethering them together stronger than any other thread of the past. She reached out and took his hand, placed it on the soft fabric of her dress just below her waist.

"You can have children, Devin," she murmured, feeling her heart catch. "I know because I'm carrying your child right now."

Devin pulled his hand away as if burned. "Don't even joke about that." He turned his shoulder to her, feeling his insides being ripped out through his heart. "Why would you be so cruel? I opened up to you. I knew you were angry, but I didn't think you'd use it against me."

Ella reached out and took his arm. "God, you're such an ass! Do you know how hard it was to say those words to you? I could never say them unless they were true. Do you know anything about me at all? Do you really think so little of me?"

He turned back, struck by the hurt ravaging her face. Her lips quivered and her eyes... Lord, her eyes. The last time he saw her look so devastated was when they'd buried her mother and she'd been left alone at the tender age of seventeen. But she couldn't possibly mean it. There had only been this morning and that one time at the cabin...

Knowledge rammed into him like an iron fist. The weekend

at the cabin had been weeks ago. Was it truly possible? Was his wife now carrying his child? He thought back to those few precious days, back further and remembered the sound of the doctor's voice when he explained the side effects of treatment.

"That can't be true."

"It can and is. I am not on the pill and you didn't ask. Neither one of us gave birth control a second thought, did we? Deplorable when you think of it in this day and age." He saw her swallow, saw honesty in her eyes. "But it was with you, and I got caught up—"

"And I didn't think it was really possible." He heard her voice this very morning, when he'd said he didn't have a condom... It didn't matter. Not because she was protected but because she was already pregnant. Oh Lord. "You're sure?"

"I did a test. And I saw a doctor shortly after that. We were abysmally irresponsible."

Their marriage was an utter and complete mess. He was working close to seventy hours a week and still lived with the specter of the tumor coming back. And yet the knowledge that Ella was carrying his baby filled him with a warmth he couldn't describe. Irresponsible be damned. It was a hell of a miracle.

He moved forward, covered her belly completely with his wide palm. "There's no bump here yet. Doesn't it seem impossible?"

She nodded at him, and he noticed she was blinking and swallowing at a rapid rate. "Impossible is precisely how I described it to my friend, Amy. Fortunately she has a cooler head than me. She informed me unprotected sex could indeed result in a pregnancy."

"You're not happy about it." The bubble of elation burst, leaving a void in its wake.

"Oh, Devin, it's more complicated than being happy or not.
160

We're a mess, you and I. And the truth is this baby shouldn't change anything between us."

His jaw dropped. "How can you say such a thing? It changes everything!" He gripped her upper arms. "This morning, when you felt faint...the sparkling water at dinner... I never would have guessed." Something else glimmered on the edges of his mind. "Why did you come? Why invite me here tonight? Was it for the story or to tell me about the baby?"

She didn't reply but stepped away from his hands, her cheeks coloring as she looked away.

Disappointment slid through his belly. He kept hoping she was the same old Ella he'd fallen in love with, but time and time again he was hit with the fact that she had goals and they consistently didn't include him. She *was* after the story. It certainly told him where he ranked in the overall scheme of things.

"If this was about your job, then I have to ask." Dread of her answer was heavy, but he had to know. "Were you *ever* going to tell me about the baby? Or were you going to write your feature and go on your merry way, leaving me none the wiser?"

"It's not like that," she said weakly, pressing her fingers to her cheeks.

"God, you were." Devin huffed out a breath of disgust. Had he allowed himself to be played again? What in hell did she want? She claimed she wanted to be free, but she melted in his arms. She said she was after the story, but she dropped the bombshell that she was pregnant. He narrowed his eyes and watched as she crossed to her chair, picked up her water and drank. Her hand was shaking.

"I don't know what I want anymore," she whispered, putting down the glass and resting her hands on the edge of the table, her fingers splayed on the linen.

His mouth tasted bitter as he swallowed. "But you weren't planning on telling me about the baby tonight." Damn, just saying the words caused his heart to take a little leap. The baby. His baby. Their baby, for God's sake. He'd all but given up on having children. And now here he was, with fatherhood in the future and with a woman he had loved, maybe still loved, if he could figure out exactly who she was.

"I suggest you figure out what it is you do want." He heard the harsh words and pressed his lips together. "If you weren't going to tell me about the baby, you must have had a plan. Let's hear it."

"Don't." Ella closed her eyes and he saw her bottom lip tremble, heard how her voice seemed to thicken with tears she seemed determined not to shed. Well, at least that was a bonus. He'd believed her tears for him earlier. He wasn't sure he was buying this time around.

And still, he waited for her response, clenching his fingers into a fist and releasing them again.

Ella took a deep breath, trying to sort out her thoughts and feelings. Right now they were all running amok in her head and heart and were not making any sense. His simple question— what did she want—was so complicated and tangled it was impossible to answer. But she knew she had to try.

So she swallowed back the tears that seemed to sit right on the edge of her eyelids, waiting for one blink that would send them down her cheeks. She'd cried more tears over Devin in the last weeks than she had when she'd left him the first time. Now that the truth was out they had to deal with it.

"I wasn't planning on telling you tonight, no."

His jaw tightened and she saw his eyes light with what she could only guess was anger but somehow sharper. "But I was going to tell you Dev. Once the dust settled from this story."

His harsh laugh cut into her as he went to the window and stared out over the deepening night. "Of course. The story first. Poor Devin. It does make good copy, doesn't it, Ella? The poor boy with cancer who recovers, gets rich and pays it forward. Real heartstrings moments. It should sell lots of copies. I bet you're hoping it'll get picked up nationally, right? Then you were going to come to me and tell me about your next project."

"I already said I wouldn't exploit you in the story!"

He spun to face her, accusing. "And I should believe you because...you've been so truthful this far?"

The words stung as they lashed out at her. "I have always been truthful," she replied, unable to fight back the heat that was rising within her as her emotions surged. They had both made mistakes. Couldn't he see that? "I might not have done it face-to-face, but at least I told you how I felt. When I came back I told you what I wanted—a divorce. One which, I might mention, you agreed to give me and sent me back to Denver with the papers unsigned. Do you really want to talk deceit to me, Devin McQuade? You hid your illness from me, and the weekend I spent here you hid your livelihood as well. You falsely represented yourself to me, and because I waited until seeing you in person—which again, I mention as that was your main gripe last time—you are angry that the first words out of my mouth weren't *congratulations daddy.*"

"You were too busy engineering things the way you wanted them!"

"I was doing my job! Can you say the same? And engineering... You, you are the one who has held my life hostage for over a decade with your refusal to give me a divorce."

"I wanted you to ask me to my face."

"Which I did," she replied, feeling slightly sick. Her blood was pumping and she was frightened, not of him but of the intensity of their situation. This should be a happy moment, but instead it was rife with blame and hostility. "I did ask you the night of the auction. And what you've done is punish me, over and over again. I hope it's been worth it."

He had the grace to look shocked and chastened. All the fight went out of her and she gripped the back of her chair, sinking into it. Her feet felt numb and she leaned forward, resting her elbows on her knees and her head in her hands.

He was at her side in a moment. "Ella? What is it? Is it the baby?" He knelt beside her chair, putting a wide, warm hand on her leg.

"Leave me alone, Devin."

"I can't do that. Not now. Not when my baby is at stake."

At that moment, Ella's heart disintegrated into dust. His concern wasn't for her. It was for the baby. The moments they had shared—that had been nothing more than nostalgic aberrations. He had wanted to punish her for leaving. He had just admitted it. He'd only fooled himself into believing he wanted to work things out. His words had held the real truth. He'd said he'd rather argue with her than not talk at all, and would rather make love than argue. What sort of a relationship was that? It needed to be built on mutual love and respect. And it was clear those were two words he did not connect with her.

Now they were joined forever through the tiny, precious life she was carrying. And Devin would not let her walk away. She knew it as sure as she knew the sky was blue. Settling was not an option. He was right. She did need a plan, and she was in no shape to present one to him now.

"I just need some rest," she murmured behind her hands, liking the feel of his palm on her knee and hating herself for it.

"I'm tired."

"I don't trust you."

She lifted her head to find Dev's close to her own, his eyes dark and earnest. "Thanks so much."

"I don't trust you not to run away again. And we need to talk about this. Both of us have been swamped with information tonight, and I understand you want to take time to assimilate it all. But I'm afraid to leave you and discover you're gone in the morning."

"I promise I won't go."

"I've heard your promises before."

The candles were burning low, and the smell of the remnants of dinner caused a thickness at the back of her throat. "Touché. But I'm not stupid. I know if I tried to take off, you'd find me. Now you have a reason to."

It hurt like hell to admit it. But the baby would motivate him like she hadn't been able to.

"Ella..."

"I don't want to argue anymore. I don't want to rehash the past and trade blame, okay? I just want to take tonight to sleep on it. I'll come see you tomorrow."

He stood, finally letting go of her leg, and the skin on her thigh cooled quickly, missing the contact. How in the world had they managed to end up here?

"I'll be out at the cabin. It's the weekend. I spend my downtime there, fishing and looking after the stock."

It was a reminder of how foolish she'd felt, discovering the truth. Making assumptions about him. She wondered if she'd see the small house in the same way now.

"I'll meet you there mid-morning."

He nodded and stacked their dirty dishes on a cart. "I'll

leave this outside on my way out."

"Thank you."

He paused, the cart in the hall, the door to the room half open.

"Don't think of running away this time."

The door shut with a quiet click and Ella wilted in the chair. Run? There was nowhere to run *to*.

Now she had twelve hours to come up with a new plan. She closed her eyes, remembering the vows she'd made to Devin and to herself all those years ago. Some she'd broken, some she hadn't. Now she had to find away to keep the most important one of all—being a good mother to her child.

Chapter Eleven

She was so not ready for this.

The rental car bounced over the dirt lane as Ella made her way back up to the cabin, hoping the makeup she'd applied covered the dark circles beneath her eyes. It had been a long night. She'd fallen asleep soon after Devin had gone, utterly exhausted by the evening's emotional rollercoaster. But she'd awakened at five, unable to stop the wheels in her head from turning as she looked out her window over the empty, dark street. Somehow she had to come up with a way they could make this work, a way to keep their baby from paying for their foolish mistakes. It was difficult to do that knowing she would have to sacrifice some dreams of her own.

By seven she'd phoned down for some tea and toast, hoping it would settle her roiling stomach. She had a shower while waiting and was feeling nearly human when the food arrived. It had only taken one half-slice of the buttered bread to turn her stomach, and she'd spent ten minutes with her head in the toilet. The joys of early pregnancy. She only hoped that the information she'd read so far was right—that within another few months, the nausea would go away. It was hard to be strong and logical when you were afraid you were going to throw up on your shoes.

In a few months, she wouldn't even be able to see her

shoes.

She bumped to a halt beside Dev's old truck. Taking a deep breath, she reached down to the passenger seat and slid one more soda cracker from the sleeve. At least these put something in her belly and seemed to agree with her.

Her knock on the door went unanswered, so she took a few moments to explore, now with new eyes. The last time she'd been here she'd looked at this place as a symbol of the rut she would have found herself in. She'd regarded it with scornful eyes, a symbol that justified all her reasons for leaving. But that wasn't true. Her assumptions about Devin had been all wrong, and she took a breath, allowing herself to enjoy the quiet and solitude. She understood why Devin had kept it as a weekend retreat. She too had adored it when they'd lived here, poor as church mice and desperately in love. It was a hideaway, away from the hustle and bustle, the noise of the real world.

The crisp fall air was refreshing, bracing, clearing her head of the cobwebs of heavy thoughts. She could do this. It was the right thing. It made sense and required equal sacrifice on both sides. After all the water under the bridge, she knew compromise was the right thing.

The path to the barn was well-trod and she walked along it, scattering leaves that looked like gold coins with her steps. She was happy she'd bought the jeans and heavy sweater yesterday as she folded her arms, encased in the soft wool. The chocolate brown collar cradled her jaw, keeping her warm and comfortable against the fall chill. She was nearly to the faded barn when she heard his voice, echoing on the light breeze. She detoured around the side to the large corral.

He was astride a gorgeous bay, oblivious to her approach. The cowboy hat she'd seen that first night at Ruby's was back on his head, shadowing the top half of his face and creating an epicenter of awareness in the pit of her stomach. Straight and tall, he sat in the saddle, faded jeans with a rip in one knee, sitting a trot effortlessly. A denim shirt hung over a fencepost. His upper half was clad only in a white T-shirt.

Where was the ruthless businessman of yesterday, who had locked the door and made love to her on his desk? Where was the deathly ill boy she'd pictured last night as he told her the truth about his cancer? This man, the one taking the horse through its paces, was the one she'd always pictured in her daydreams. This was the man she'd stayed away from for twelve long years. And with good reason. This man was dangerous. Irresistible. This man, more than any other, had the power to change her mind. For a moment her resolve faltered, simply by watching him.

He turned a corner and saw her standing there, back from the fence, and his body seemed to pause. He reined the bay in to a walk, made his way close to where she was standing, his hips swaying with the movement of the gait. She bit down on her lip. She knew before he spoke what he would sound like, knew before he dismounted how he would smell, feel. Her plan was sound but not without flaws. She wasn't immune to Dev.

"So I don't have to go chasing after all." The words were said lightly, but he didn't smile.

"I told you I'd be here." Her voice came out with a slight squeak and she cleared her throat. The saltines had made her throat dry, and now that the morning had waned she suddenly wished for a glass of milk.

"Let me put this guy up, and I'll meet you at the house."

He swung his leg over the saddle and dismounted, giving a little hop and gripping the reins with a hand. Ella took one look at the jeans and swallowed. He'd been irresistible in his suit yesterday. Faded, shaped-to-his-body jeans took that up a whole other level.

She nodded and turned her back, hurrying back up the path. Where had this physical *need* for him come from? Sure, her hormones were out of whack but this was ridiculous. She detoured to the car for the rest of the crackers and took them inside the cabin. She peeked in the fridge, finding no white milk but a small container of chocolate. Her mouth watered and stomach rumbled. She got a glass from the cupboard—the same one she'd put their dishes in after they'd married—and poured the liquid into it. She smiled as she drank, the cool richness of it soothing her throat and tummy.

She'd rinsed her glass and put it in the drying rack when he came up the steps, stopping outside to remove his boots. Ella smoothed her hands down the front of her sweater, nervous all over again. He had to listen. He simply had to. Surely he would see her solution was best for everyone, if he could put aside his foolish notion of pride long enough to think about it.

"Sorry for the wait."

He wasn't quite comfortable, she could tell. He kept his words carefully modulated, intentional. It seemed they were both on their best behavior today, which was good. If they could tread carefully, avoid setting each other off, maybe then he'd see the benefits to her plan.

"It's no trouble. We didn't set an exact time."

"Did you sleep?" He took a step forward, paused by the table. "You look tired."

She smiled a little, cursing the black smudges beneath her eyes, thinking that maybe it wouldn't hurt to share a little of the pregnancy with him. If he knew how heavily her life was affected by the changes going on he might accept her conditions more readily.

"I slept until about five, but then I had to use the bathroom. I couldn't sleep after that, so I ordered up some toast and had a shower. The toast didn't settle so well..." She paused, softening as she looked up into his face. "It's been an eventful morning."

"You've been morning sick?"

"Not so much. Mostly just nauseous or needing to eat like yesterday when I got faint. This morning though... I think I just had a lot on my mind."

"You need to take better care of yourself," he deemed. "Can I get you anything?"

She bit back a retort at his directive. She *was* taking good care of herself and this baby. She'd followed her books to the letter. There was no point in sniping at him. His solicitousness was touching because she knew it was sincere. Insincerity was definitely not one of his faults, even when the truth was unpleasant. She knew he believed every single word he said. The problem was he believed it so strongly that he couldn't see the other side.

She needed him to see the other side today.

"I'm fine. But I'll take your ear, Dev. I thought long and hard about what we should do, and I think I've come up with a solution."

"I'll listen. But at the end you need to listen to me too."

"Agreed." She twisted her fingers nervously, knowing he would never agree to every detail of her plan. She had to expect he'd present his own side, and somehow in the middle they'd find something that worked. They had to.

Ella sat in the hard-backed kitchen chair, taking a deep breath and mentally reciting the words she'd put together on the drive from the hotel. Devin poured himself a glass of water from the tap and came to sit across from her. He was a combination of the focused office Dev and the devil-may-care cowboy. The combination was hard to resist. But that was the very reason she had to make him see sense.

She stifled an anxious laugh—*let the negotiations begin.* And from the success of Dev's business over the years, she guessed he was pretty good at getting what he wanted.

"I think the most important thing right now is to not think about what I want or what you want but to think about what is best for the baby. I don't want this baby to grow up like I did, Devin. I want this baby to feel loved, and wanted, and secure."

"I agree."

Relief flooded her—the first hurdle behind her. "And I think we are both going to have to make sacrifices to make sure that happens."

"Absolutely."

Agreement again. This was almost too easy, and it made her even more nervous rather than soothed. And now the hard part—the particulars. This would be the hardest sell, because his pride would take a hit. And he'd agreed so readily she knew he had to have his own ideas of what they should do. She swallowed and pinned what she hoped was a believable smile on her face.

"I want to keep the baby, and I want you to be involved in his or her life. Our child needs to know you as a father and a constant in its life, and it needs a mother and father who are committed to providing him or her with the best life we possibly can."

"I'm so glad to hear you say that," Devin said, the words tumbling out. He reached across the table and took her cold hand in his, warming it with the firm pressure. "Last night when I said what I did about tearing up the divorce papers, I was sure you would run the other direction. I'm glad you've thought about it and—"

"Stop," she commanded, the seed of worry now a hard ball of anxiety. "That's *not* what I'm saying, Dev. I still want the divorce."

"What?" The pressure on her hand tightened as his gaze caught hers, wide with surprise and dismay.

"I don't think our staying married is in the best interest of the baby."

He let go of her hand and spun in his chair, rising from the table in a single, harsh motion. "You just said you didn't want the baby raised like you were. I know it was hard being the child of a single mother. I know you were left alone a lot while she tried to make ends meet, and I know how you wanted a father. We talked about all this, Ella, when we talked about getting married. I didn't forget. How can you accept less now? This baby deserves a mother and father."

He was right about all of it. This wasn't the ideal situation they'd dreamed of. But she'd come to learn life rarely was ideal.

"There's a big difference, Dev. You won't leave us high and dry the way my father did. You'll be there, you'll support us, you'll be involved. To stay married... Do you want to bring our child up in a house with two parents who don't love each other?" The words echoed through the cabin. She wouldn't deny him a place in his own child's life, but she wouldn't open herself up to hurt again either. She understood now that the years since their split had been one big test she'd failed. She couldn't spend her life wondering if she measured up. Waiting to fail again.

And yet part of her longed to hear him deny it. To have him say he did love her. But how could he? All they had truly done since reconnecting was fight, share a few memories and have mind-blowing sex. It wasn't enough and they both knew it.

"Isn't having a baby reason enough to try to work at it? What better reason is there?" He braced his hands on the back of his chair, his lips pulled taut as the tension in the room seemed to multiply, thick and heavy.

Her eyes smarted. He was already so invested in this tiny life and he'd known about it for less than twenty-four hours. "How can you put the burden of a marriage on such tiny shoulders, Devin? How can you ask a baby to be responsible for the success or failure of a marriage when we've already screwed it up so spectacularly on our own?"

The starch went out of his body and he resumed his chair again, running a hand through his hair, leaving one side standing slightly on end. She watched him sadly. At one time discovering they were expecting a child would have been the happiest moment of their lives. Now it was bittersweet and fraught with recriminations and sad wishes.

"What do you suggest, then? Because I get the feeling you have a proposal up your sleeve."

She leaned forward, squeezing her hands between her knees. "You sign the divorce papers. In return, I will give up the job in Boston and stay in Denver, and we share the parenting. Durango and Denver aren't that far apart. The baby will stay with me, but you'll be able to visit anytime you like, and I fully expect you'll want to have visits here at your home too. Our baby needs a father, Dev. What he or she doesn't need is living with a bad example of a marriage, don't you agree?"

Devin stared at her, unable to think of the right response. Yes, he agreed, but the plan he had in his head didn't include a bad marriage. It included them working things out. Putting the pieces back together. Now that their fears and insecurities had been laid on the table, surely they could put it all behind them and move forward. The news that he was going to be a father was so incredible that he had been sure things would turn out right. Why would such a thing happen if it weren't to bring them together again?

And he didn't want to be a part-time father. He wanted to be there for every precious moment, the way his parents had been there for him. The way Ella's father had never been there for her. As he stared into her earnest face, he realized he wanted that not only for himself, not only for their baby, but for her too. To somehow make up for the pieces that had been missing. Looking back, maybe that was where they'd gone wrong. He'd tried to do it when they were kids, and he had failed. Now their own child was at stake too, and he couldn't push away the need to fix it. Even if she didn't like it.

"And if I don't divorce you?"

"I will still go through with it, and you will have to contest it in court. Then I expect there will be custody issues to settle." He stared at her, not quite believing she'd go that far. But Ella was determined. She'd walked away once before without looking back, hadn't she?

"I don't want that, Devin," she continued, her face softening. "I want us to do this as friends, for the sake of our child. I'm not asking you to give up much."

Not much? At this moment it felt like he was giving up *everything*. He no longer cared about revenge or secrets. She was asking him to give up on their marriage once and for all. She was asking him to give up time with a child he already loved. Not to mention the dream they'd had of a two-parent family. She was taking away his chance to make things right.

"You mean my life will mostly stay unchanged."

"Yes, of course." She smiled a little, like she was trying to be encouraging.

"What if I don't want it to stay unchanged? You are asking me to make sacrifices—as a husband and a parent." He thought of visits every other weekend and separate vacations. He thought of her marrying later and another man stepping in to be a father to his child. The very idea nearly ripped his heart from his chest. "I can't do it, Ell. It's too much to ask."

"Too much?" Her gaze snapped up to his, her cheekbones flushed as a thin line of tension underscored the words. "You get to keep your business, the life you've built here. Would you be willing to give up DMQ and go to Boston with me? What about me, Devin? I wanted this Boston job. I wanted the promotion and the new life. I'm willing to give it up so that *you* can be close to the baby. So you can be a father, and we can work together. Do you think I wanted to stay at the paper forever?"

The idea of giving up DMQ and moving across the country was ludicrous. He could support them all on what DMQ brought in. His parents were here, his child's grandparents. An aunt and uncle and cousins.

"My family is here. How can I deny my parents the chance to be grandparents to our baby?"

Ella's lips tightened. "Because this is about us and not them, Devin."

He thought of the typewriter and the wistful look on her face that Saturday morning when she'd run her fingers over the keyboard. "If we truly did this together, you wouldn't have to stay at the paper. You could write the book you always said you wanted to. Hell, Ella, I can support us all with DMQ." The idea sounded so perfect to his ears his imagination took flight. "We could even renovate this place, use it on weekends. I could bring our son or daughter here and teach them how to ride and fish and you could type away..."

For a long, quiet moment, he saw uncertainty on her face. She was tempted. But the hesitation was quickly masked and she merely offered a distant, polite smile.

"That's a lovely fantasy, Devin, but it's missing one important element. It would require a strong relationship as a foundation, and that's one we don't have. There's too much resentment in both of us."

It was difficult to argue when what she was saying sounded so damned logical. He could see her—and his baby—slipping through his fingers and there wasn't a damned thing he could do about it. She had made up her mind. She'd made it up years ago, and he hadn't accepted it. Now look where they'd ended up. How could he ask his child to pay the price for his pride, their mistakes? He rose from the chair and went out on the small verandah, needing desperately to breathe in some of the cool, clean air. Everything was closing around him. He hadn't been able to say anything to change her mind, and he felt small when she looked at him with disappointment in her eyes.

He closed his eyes. That was it, wasn't it? He'd been so afraid of disappointing her that he'd shut her out instead.

But what more did she want? He was prepared to give them the best life he possibly could.

When she followed him he opened his eyes and rested his hands on the railing, staring down over the valley below.

"Dev," she murmured, putting her hand on his arm.

Before he could change his mind, he gripped her fingers in his opposite hand, turned and pulled her close, pressing his lips to hers.

Her lips parted beneath his, soft and sweet and a taste he knew like it was the air he breathed. Her body touched his and he thought of the miracle of their child resting between them. How could he let her go, feeling the way he was feeling? He knew now that he loved her; he'd never stopped. But their love was so complicated that saying it—that simple declaration—was beyond him. She'd never believe him. She'd think he was saying it to get his way.

He dropped light kisses on the crest of her cheek. "Does this feel like goodbye to you?"

Then he heard her breath catch. Her lips were close to his ear when she whispered back, "No. But it's not enough."

As the kiss waned, he rested his forehead against hers, the elation he'd felt leaking away like a deflated balloon. He knew she hadn't lied when she said she'd fight him. And a court battle was not what he wanted.

"If you ever loved me, Dev, you'll let me go."

He pulled away, feeling as bereft now as he had the day he'd received her letter calling their marriage a mistake. For over a decade she'd been asking him to do this. Perhaps it was time. Time to let go and face past mistakes. To make a clean slate of it. He stepped back until no part of his body was touching her, but not quite out of the cloud of her clean, floral scent. For an odd second, he knew he'd remember it for the rest of his life, the soft scent of goodbye. He knew her well enough to know she meant what she said. And he knew sometimes the best thing was to lose a battle so you could fight another day.

"I'll have my lawyer draw up new papers first thing Monday morning, as well as a custody agreement and financial support."

Her lips fell open and surprise widened her eyes. "You mean that."

"A court battle isn't good for you or the baby. Maybe it's time I started listening."

"I'm sorry—"

"Don't," he ordered, unable to look at her any longer. He strode past her to the door. "For God's sake, don't apologize. Don't say anything more. Please."

He went back inside, feeling caged within the four walls where they'd first lived during their marriage. He waited until he heard her car leave the drive. Then he put on his boots, grabbed his hat and headed back to the barn.

Chapter Twelve

Ella pressed send and sighed, feeling a sense of relief that the article was done and now on its way to her editor. It had been a struggle, sifting through all she'd learned and finding the angle she'd wanted. Finally, it had clicked into place and her fingers had flown over the keys—a story not about politics or profit but about people. A story vastly different from the one she was assigned. She had to be crazy. Her hopes of the Boston job were gone. She had traded them in for a bigger goal—two available parents for her unborn child. To turn in something other than her assignment wouldn't do her job security any favors. And yet she had to write the story her conscience told her to write. She would deal with the consequences.

She was just shutting down her laptop when a knock sounded. She opened the door to her apartment, surprised to see a courier standing with a clipboard and a large envelope.

"Ella McQuade?"

She swallowed, nodded mutely, more affected than she cared to admit by the use of her married name. She signed her name next to the appropriate number and accepted the package.

It was from a legal firm in Durango.

Dev had remained true to his word, though after the scene at the cabin she had known he would. With trembling fingers she opened the envelope and withdrew the thick sheaf of papers. Divorce, custody. His signature, finally. All that was left was for her to sign and file them with the court.

She scanned the sheets, reading the terms, relieved to see he had stuck to the conditions she'd laid out last Saturday morning. Nor had he wasted any time. She wanted to feel relieved, but all she could manage was a gaping sense of loss. The young, idealistic girl, the handsome, ambitious boy... This was what they had come to. Co-parenting in two different cities.

Before she could change her mind, she grabbed a pen and signed her name beneath his, the letters blurred through her tears.

Ella stood before Charlie's desk, her teeth clenched as he finished writing something on a paper. He was keeping her waiting. On purpose. He knew it and she knew it. Just as she knew what was coming was not going to be pleasant.

Without looking at her, he spoke. "Sit down, Ella."

She felt her stomach turn, a mix of nerves and the morning sickness that hadn't yet cleared. "I think I'd rather stand, sir."

Finally Donovan looked up at her. He reached to his side and picked up a paper. "This is what you're handing in?"

"Yes, sir." She worked hard at schooling her features. Donovan had to see a strong, determined woman. Not one whose knees were trembling. She'd known there would likely be backlash at the fact she hadn't written the story he wanted. And she'd thought she'd be okay with it. Until the moment she'd been summoned to his office.

"What am I supposed to do with it?"

"Print it, sir." Her heart took a little leap, rather proud at her assertiveness.

"Print it?"

Donovan's voice didn't sound amused at her temerity and her internal smile waned.

"This isn't what you were assigned, Ella. There is no news here. This is a touchy-feely editorial sadly lacking in newsworthy facts. What happened to screwing HMOs to the post? What happened to putting the spotlight on one of Colorado's most successful entrepreneurs?" He tossed the article on his desk with a negligent flick of the wrist. "This doesn't sell papers."

And that was, she knew, the whole point. To sell papers. Up until a week ago she had agreed with him.

But not now.

"It's the truth, Charlie. That's all I can say."

"It has to be rewritten."

Her heart stopped for one brief second, and she was afraid she wouldn't be able to find her voice. "No," she answered, the word weak and thready.

"Come on. I'm giving you another chance here. Rewrite it by tomorrow and it can still feature in the weekend edition. You're a good reporter, Ella. Your talents have been wasted, and I put my faith in you with this assignment."

"I know that." She saw a vision of her dreams going down the toilet and considered doing what he asked. She needed this job. If she wasn't going to Boston now she had to make a name for herself here.

"Then what in the world possessed you to write this? The first installment was wonderful, thought provoking, inflammatory. I really thought you'd nailed it."

She had, and she knew it. And then she had a vision of Betty's face as she'd spoken of Devin's help, and of Devin's when he'd told her about his cancer. "I wrote the first article on face value," she tried to explain. "But I couldn't this time. This is about real people, Charlie. I can't advance by stepping on others. I just can't."

"Why? Because you're married to Devin McQuade?"

Ella's jaw dropped. "You know about that?"

He nodded. "Of course I do. I have for some time. You forget I was once a junior reporter. With research skills."

He'd known and he'd sent her to cover the story anyway. If it had been intentional, it was cruel. She'd been tested in so many ways from so many corners, and she'd failed at each one. Well, no more. This time she would do what was right. She would not change her story. She had done the right thing writing it the way she had. If she was sure of nothing else, she was sure of that.

"My story stands," she claimed, straightening her shoulders, feeling at once proud with an underbelly of uncertainty.

"If that's your position, I'm afraid we have a problem. There is a reason we call them 'assignments'. You write what you're told to write, with a clear expectation of what that will be." His amiable face hardened. There had been enough beating around the bush, apparently. Charlie was ready to play hardball.

"I can't work that way. So yes, we have a problem. Are you going to print the article or not?"

"Yes," he acceded, sighing and leaning back in his chair. "Yes, I'm going to print it. But as an editorial piece."

"Thank you." She turned to leave, needing to end the conversation. She needed to think, and his words were warring with Devin's at the moment. How could she be force-fed the kind of stories she would write? What was the alternative? If she stayed one more minute, she would throw away her career with one thoughtless remark. No, she needed time. Time to think it through.

"Ella—"

"I'll get back to you about the rest, Charlie. Just give me the afternoon, okay?"

His eyes held a measure of understanding and disappointment she couldn't bear to see. She left his office quickly, closing the door behind her, heading straight for her cubicle and feeling ill once more. This time it had nothing to do with the life growing inside her.

Devin couldn't bring himself to go to the cabin, not this weekend. The memory of being there the last time still left a sour taste. He paid Frank overtime to look after the stock in his absence, and when he couldn't stand the quiet in his condo anymore, went to the Animas Resort for Sunday breakfast and then out to the river. He took his rod with him. The best fishing would soon be over. He did his best thinking when he was fishing, nothing but the silence and the rhythm of his wrist as he cast out with the fly.

He found a good lie and quietly entered the water, feeling the cool liquid pool around his waders. As he cast, hearing the zing of the line through the reel, he remembered the first time he'd seen Ella again. She'd accused him of never looking forward, of being stuck in the cabin and wasting his time fishing and watching ball games. She'd been wrong. It wasn't a waste, but a way to unwind from work, to burn off stress. To remember—and appreciate—where he'd come from. But she'd been right in one way. He'd held on to some things too long. He hadn't left her behind. Now that he had, it was more painful than he expected.

He got a few nibbles, but the trout weren't biting well and he was far too distracted. He packed up his gear and made the trek back to the resort. It had been one of DMQ's most recent acquisitions, and while he trusted the running of it to Kate McGrew, he enjoyed being onsite and keeping on top of things. It had been an enjoyable revelation—to discover his passion went beyond the initial acquisition stage. He had thought he'd buy properties and flip them, but instead he invested in them, fixing them up. He made them profitable and reaped the benefits.

He went into the lounge to grab a sandwich for lunch. He'd ordered and was sipping on a Coors when Kate slid into the booth with him. "Hey, stranger."

He grinned up at her pretty face. "Hey yourself. Business looks good." He looked around the room, noting the busy tables and smiling staff. "You're doing a hell of a job, Katie. I don't know if I've said that lately, but it's true."

"It keeps me out of trouble."

"I'm sorry about that."

They shared a good-natured smile and a waitress put a glass of ice water in front of Kate. He had never seen her take a drink on the job, not even when it was more social than work. Hiring her had been possibly the best business decision he'd made in turning the resort around.

She was a good friend, and he wondered if he'd overlooked an opportunity there. The night of the auction she'd bid right along with Ella until the last. Would their forty-eight hours have been more than he expected?

Would he have wanted it to be?

"Last time I saw you," she noted, pushing her straw through her water, "you had your shirt off and a bunch of horny women were howling."

He blushed. "Thanks for bringing that up."

"It was quite a show."

He met her gaze. She wasn't hiding or flirting. Instead, her brown eyes met his evenly, perhaps even with a hint of challenge.

"You did some bidding yourself. I don't think I ever thanked you for that. You did me a favor."

The warmth in her eyes cooled. "It wasn't completely altruistic, you know."

Devin tried, wished he felt some attraction, some pull to Kate that would take his mind off of Ella. It would make things so much easier if he could find himself interested in someone else. But it was no use. He looked away.

"That's okay, Devin. I gave up on more a long time ago."

He swiveled his head back to stare at her. Kate? In all the years he'd known her, he hadn't realized she'd fostered feelings for him. The first night they'd met he'd embarrassed himself by inflicting a sloppy, drunken kiss on her lips. Her no-nonsense response had solidified a friendship. Or so he thought.

"Kate, I don't know what to say."

Kate took a sip of her water and put the glass back down on the table, creating a new wet ring on the wood surface. "Hell, the whole town knows there's never been anyone besides Ella for you. How are things with her, anyway?"

He puckered his brow, feeling the jump of his pulse at the mention of her name, followed by the sinking knowledge that it was really over between them. "Why would you ask?"

Kate sat back against the green padded cushions of the booth. "Rumor has it she checked into the Strater last week."

"The rumor mill is working just fine, I see." Irritation flared and he pushed his beer away. "I suppose everyone knows she's pregnant too."

"Dammit!" Kate dribbled cold water down her blouse front as her lips fell open. She grabbed a napkin and blotted the white fabric. "Jeez, Devin. You might warn a girl. Seriously? I suppose now is the time I should offer congratulations."

Devin shook his head. Kate had been a friend for a long time. He'd never really clued into the attraction thing, but he'd always been able to talk to her, beginning with the night he'd made his first real-estate deal and the celebrating had turned into a bourbon-fuelled lament about his broken heart. The kiss had been an inauspicious beginning to long friendship and then business relationship. Telling her about this now was just as embarrassing, considering what they'd just said—and what they hadn't.

"Not exactly. Our divorce was filed this week too."

For several long seconds Kate looked at him, making him feel like she was somehow measuring. Go ahead, let her, he thought. It wasn't like he hadn't been doing the same thing all week and finding himself coming up short.

"So you become a bachelor and a dad all in the same week? Interesting." She tapped a fingernail on the table. "Very interesting."

"I'm glad you think so."

She laughed, then reached over and patted his arm. "You haven't seen the paper today, have you?"

He shook his head, wondering why Kate was suddenly looking at him like she was the cat that got the cream. The earlier tension was gone and she was back to being just his friend again.

"I've been fishing."

She slid out of the booth and went to a table next to the

entrance. When she came back, she opened the Sunday edition, folded it in half and passed it across the table.

It was the story. Her story. Ella's. He'd wondered what she was going to write, hoping she'd meant it when she said she wouldn't use his illness for her own gain. His picture was there though, the color one they'd used in that magazine article a few months ago, and a headline—*Healthcare for Real People.*

His lip curled as he realized what she'd done—put him front and center. He'd trusted her, dammit. He'd given her what she wanted—a divorce. He'd agreed to her arrangement even though it was the last thing he wanted. And now here he was, in print. He refolded the paper and handed it back, keeping a rein on his anger and forcing his face to remain neutral in Kate's presence. Maybe Ella had been right all along. This was a better way, making the split between them official and permanent. But it hurt that she'd betrayed his trust again. So much for not exploiting him.

"Now you understand the bachelor part," he growled, looking away from Kate and taking a drink. "This wasn't supposed to happen."

When Kate said nothing he turned his head back. She was watching him with a puzzled expression.

"What do you mean, understand the bachelor part?"

"Ella's not the same girl I married, Kate. I don't think I know her at all. And just when I think I do, she up and does something to reinforce my original opinion."

She pushed the paper back across the table and got up. "Maybe you need to read the article, Devin, rather than jumping to conclusions. I've got work. Let me know if you need anything."

He waited until she was out the door before picking up the newspaper. His heart pounded for some undefined reason as he opened the editorial section once more.

There it was, with a picture of him, and another of Betty Tucker. His eyes scanned the print.

Healthcare for Real People
Ella Turner, Columnist

Last month I brought you a story about Betty Tucker and how our healthcare system—and the capitalist structure of our insurance companies—has failed her. Today I was planning on continuing that story with numbers and facts and, let's face it, making an example of her plight in her fight for cancer treatment.

But that's not the story I'm bringing you today because healthcare isn't about dollars and cents, profit and loss. Nor is it about who gets to decide which treatments are available to patients. Doctors should be the ones making those decisions, not bureaucrats in high-rise offices. Healthcare is about people.

Life is about people, when it comes right down to it.

Devin McQuade, a business owner in Betty's town of Durango, has stepped up and paid for Betty's treatment out of his own pocket. He didn't do this for personal gain. He didn't do it for recognition or to buy himself good favor with karma. In fact, he would have preferred that I not bring the matter to your attention at all. He did it for Betty. Because for Devin, it's about people and doing what's right.

Oh, that stung. She'd used the same argument in convincing him her "arrangement" was for the best. He set his teeth and read on.

It's about a woman who once called 911 when he needed it, visited him in hospital, brought him home cooking. Betty was a friend who gave what she could—her time and her caring. Devin McQuade has done nothing more than help a friend. Betty is the true hero of this story, an example of the good we want to believe is in all of us. A person who deserves the same chance of survival as someone with many more zeroes on file at the IRS.

There is no place for moral judgments or financial comparisons in healthcare. It's about equality. We're all human beings. We all have families and friends, hopes and dreams. We all deserve kindness, and compassion, and access to treatments that can make us well again.

We could debate the merits of healthcare models all day long, argue about fiscal ramifications and politics, but the truth of the matter is, none of it is important.

Perhaps if we treated all our patients as friends and gave them a face where currently a dollar sign resides, the reform we need so desperately could finally happen.

We wish a speedy recovery to Mrs. Tucker.

Devin put down the paper.

It was not the article he had expected when he first saw his picture on the page. It was conspicuously absent of details of his illness. It treated Betty with caring and respect. It had very likely landed Ella in hot water with her superiors—a short editorial piece rather than the newsworthy expose he knew she'd been assigned.

So why had she done it?

As he let out a breath, he realized he'd been testing her. Ever since her return, he'd prodded, searching for the gentle, caring Ella he remembered. He'd criticized and berated her for her choices, only seeing her through the glasses of his own hurt pride and disillusionment. And here she was, that young, soft-hearted girl that had become a strong woman. Right in this

190

short piece of writing that would never be syndicated in national papers as a hard-hitting piece of journalism. It was quiet and truthful. It wouldn't earn her any promotions, wouldn't be syndicated in big papers around the country, wouldn't open any doors.

Perhaps it had stopped mattering. Because she'd given up those dreams so they could parent their child together.

And for the first time since seeing her again, he felt like a complete and utter heel.

He read the article once more. This was the Ella he'd fallen in love with. A woman who could see the big picture, who cared about others and showed compassion. In her words he caught a glimpse of the eight-year-old girl who had hollered blue murder at a classmate who was torturing a frog and then had picked up that slimy thing and carried it to the tall grass on the side of the playground. A woman who kept her word and had exploited no one, even knowing she might bear the brunt of it professionally.

Devin put his hand over his mouth, rubbing the two-day stubble on his chin. He'd been so utterly wrong. He'd made another mistake, this one bigger than any of the others. He had signed the papers, setting her free rather than fighting for her. And why? He always fought for what he wanted—his business, all the years he'd refused a divorce. Hell, he'd fought for his life when he'd been sick.

It was only the last in a line of mistakes he'd made with her—twelve long years of jumping to conclusions, as Kate had put it. The night at the hotel Ella had admitted she'd waited for him to come after her. To fight for her. And all he'd done was demand that she be perfect, even though he'd made it impossible.

He threw a tip on to the tabletop and tucked the paper under his arm. Tomorrow morning he'd be on the commuter flight. And he'd make this right once and for all.

Ella put the potted plant down on her desk and pressed her fingers to her lower back. No one at the paper besides Amy knew about the baby. It was just as well. She'd put off enough explanations already. But from now on, that wasn't going to be a problem.

She'd thought long and hard, into the wee hours when she should have been sleeping. But the same answer kept coming back to her. This wasn't what she wanted, not anymore. Last week she'd put in her notice. Going freelance had sounded liberating at two a.m., and her idealistic side—a part of her she'd tamped down ever since her rushed marriage to Devin—thought that being able to work from a home office, at least until the baby was old enough for daycare, sounded brilliant. It was a freedom she hadn't experienced in a long time. She was the one calling the shots. She could write whatever she wanted. Whenever she wanted.

As she packed up her desk though, the idea was losing its luster. She needed to support herself. For Devin to assist with their child was one thing. But she refused to ask him for help. He'd done what she'd asked of him and she wouldn't take further advantage.

The bank box was nearly full when a tap sounded on the frame of her cubicle. "Going somewhere?"

Her body froze in the second before she looked up. All week she had thought about that voice, the rough-and-ready sexy timbre of it. Leaving the marriage behind was far easier than the man, she'd discovered. She raised her gaze and saw him leaning negligently against the thin metal frame of her cubicle door. The cheeky smile was on his face, making the single dimple pop.

"What are you doing here?"

He pushed away from the frame, and her tongue snuck out to dampen her lips. He was businessman Dev today, dressed in charcoal gray trousers and a white shirt open at the throat. His dark hair was carelessly styled and she seriously didn't know which Devin she preferred. The ultra sexy office jockey or the careless cowboy in torn jeans and boots. She might as well face it. Dev was irresistible either way. And she was going to have to get over that if they were going to be co-parenting.

"I saw your editorial."

"You could have emailed."

"Maybe I wanted to offer my congratulations." He stepped inside the tiny square space and she put the cover on the box simply to keep her hands busy.

"You'd be the only one," she muttered, searching for something to do with her hands now, incredibly ill at ease.

"It was a fine piece of writing."

"It was an editorial abysmally short on news or controversy."

Dev's voice came quietly then. "It was honest. I'm proud of you, Ella."

She swallowed roughly, fighting to keep her emotions from showing. Devin had done nothing but be negative about her choices. She shouldn't want his approval, but in her heart his words meant more than she cared to admit.

"So the box is?" He stopped in front of the small desk and put his hands in his pockets oh so casually. Ella looked into his face. There was no mockery now. He was completely serious. His face was soft with concern. It chased away her earlier thoughts and made her pride kick in.

"Today is my last day." She rested her hands atop the box and smiled, but it felt brittle.

"I know what was in the paper wasn't what you were assigned. And that's my fault. Maybe if I talk to your boss..."

"I didn't get fired. I quit. I put in my notice a week ago."

"You quit?" His hands came out of his pockets. "What happened?"

Ella looked around the office, at the open cubicles devoid of privacy. Work was going on as usual. Some of the staff had taken her out for a farewell lunch, and a good luck card was tucked into her personal items. But none of them knew the whole story, and Ella would just as soon leave without explaining.

"Can we go somewhere else? I don't want to talk about this here."

"I can take you home. I rented a car. Let me carry your things."

He picked up the box without waiting for her assent and paused, letting her lead the way through the door. Ella felt her cheeks flare, knowing eyes were on her as she left, her sexy now-ex husband carrying the contents of her desk. That he did so, clearly out of a solicitude born of her condition, made her feel both flattered and a little like she should be insisting on doing it herself.

Outside he led the way to a silver sedan and put her box in the back seat. He opened the passenger door, waiting for her to get in. "So where are we headed?"

Ella forced herself to take deep breaths. It didn't matter that he was here. And now she didn't have to walk all those blocks carrying the box. It would be fine. It would be a chance to test run the new dynamics of the relationship. They needed to establish a baseline for dealing with each other, and better to do it now before the baby arrived than later.

She gave him directions, then sat back, laying her head on the padded rest.

"How are you feeling?"

"Okay. Still queasy in the mornings, but it's bearable. Better if I have a good night's sleep actually. It's when I'm tired that it's worse." Like it had been the day she'd checked out of the Strater. Or the morning after signing the papers. She'd tossed and turned most of that night.

She pointed at the next street and Devin made a turn. "It's just here," she said, indicating a building on the right. "I picked it because it was close to everything. I can walk to just about everything I need. Grocery, dry cleaners, restaurants, theater..." It occurred to her that restaurants and theater were things she wouldn't be doing as often after the baby came. There were so many adjustments she'd be making. It wasn't that she didn't want to. It was simply that it was so...different. And she'd be doing it alone. All the changes happening and those to come seemed momentarily overwhelming.

She'd never had a great model for motherhood, and she was terrified of making mistakes.

Devin parked and got out, going around the hood and opening her door. He retrieved the box from the back seat as well. Ella took a breath. After years of going it alone, having someone do even these small favors for her felt strange. It would be so easy to get used to. And so dangerous. Having it, and losing it, was what had driven her mother to try to find it again, sinking into depression when it all went wrong time after time. She blinked, wanting to let herself love him and so afraid that if she did she'd end up just like her mother had. Heartbroken and alone with a daughter to raise.

"You never did tell me why you were here," she said, more

determined than ever that they find a way to work together.

He smiled over top of the box, and she noticed how the simple angle of carrying it emphasized the muscles in his arms. She looked away, instead digging out her key for the main door.

"Like you, I didn't want to talk about it at your office. I stopped by hoping to take you for a late lunch, but this is better."

"It is?" Her heartbeat stuttered. The idea of being alone with him wasn't something she was used to yet.

"We can talk better here."

She thought they'd pretty much covered everything the last time—certainly the divorce and custody agreements had settled the rest. But he was here and he seemed to have a purpose. "You might as well come up then."

She led him to the elevator and hit the button for the third floor. Within seconds they were at the door to her apartment. At least she didn't need to be ashamed of her home, she realized, unlocking the door and leading the way inside. The building was fairly new, the neutral-colored walls and flooring unmarked. It was small, but she'd tastefully decorated it, using black and white tones with the odd splash of color.

It didn't, however, look like a place to raise a child. Soon she'd have to start shopping for cribs and all manner of items.

"This is nice, Ell. It looks like you. Comfortable but classy."

The unexpected compliment filled her with warmth, while at the same time putting her on alert. Devin was being nice. Too nice, considering.

"Thanks. It's small, but I've been happy here."

"Have you?"

Ah, there it was. Just the tiniest note of challenge. "Yes, I think I have."

He put the box down on a drop-leaf table. "Do you want to tell me what happened at the paper? Did they force you to leave?"

Ella remembered the very awkward meeting she'd had with Charlie. For the first time ever someone had questioned her objectivity. Normally she would have felt the failure acutely. Instead, she felt proud that she'd written what she had. She had done the right thing—for Betty, for Dev. And for herself. Her sense of panic from earlier dissipated. Come what may, she knew she'd done the right thing.

"Not at all. Sure, I took some heat for the article, but it wouldn't have cost me my job. It was more...a realization, I suppose, of the kinds of things I wanted to write about rather than what I was being told to write. I was so focused on where I was going that I used my job as a vehicle, you know? And I forgot to enjoy what I was doing. Maybe letting go of the Boston opportunity was good for me, when I think about it. It made me see I wasn't really happy at the paper, and it wasn't really a stepping stone anymore."

"So you quit."

"I did."

His smile spread slowly. "That's fantastic."

The smile was contagious and she found herself answering with one of her own. "Sure. It's always great to find oneself pregnant and unemployed."

"Any plans?"

"I'm going to try freelancing for now, I guess. I can work from home until the baby is older. Now that you finally know what happened at work, will you please tell me what you're doing here?"

Devin reached out and took her hand, squeezing her fingers in his. "I came to tell you I made a big mistake, Ella."

Indecision swirled through her. "You did?"

He nodded, pulling her hand and pressing it to his chest. "I made a mistake signing those papers, and I've come to make it right."

Chapter Thirteen

Ella pulled her hand away. No, he couldn't be doing this to her now. Not now when she finally had achieved the impossible—getting him to agree to a divorce. She had worked so hard to make a new start for herself. And yet every time she thought about it, Devin snuck into her thoughts and dreams. He couldn't be changing his mind now, could he? She forced herself to take a few clearing breaths. "It is too late, Devin. The papers have been signed and registered with the court. We *are* divorced."

"I know. It doesn't matter."

Hope fluttered and she frowned, annoyed that she was reacting this way. She had to think with her head. Her heart wasn't trustworthy. She had to stand on her own two feet. Devin kept changing his mind about what he wanted. But with the courts, it was as final as it was going to get. He couldn't hold it over her any longer.

"What do you mean, it doesn't matter? Of course it does. Our marriage is over. And divorcing wasn't a mistake. We needed to do it so we can focus on just being parents." Desperation slipped into her voice. Co-parenting was going to be difficult enough. They had to find a way to put their lingering feelings aside, not only for the sake of their child but for themselves too. She realized what she needed from Devin was what he'd been in the beginning—that one person she could rely on, talk to, go to when she was in trouble. And that person was slipping away with each moment. "We *agreed*, Devin. It's for the best for all of us."

"I know." He refused to rise to her challenge. On the contrary, he seemed so very sure of himself it was scaring her. Because she wasn't sure at all. She'd missed him horribly since coming back to Denver. She'd cried the day the papers had been filed. On the surface she could say it was hormones. In her heart she knew what it was, and right now it was hurting her—deeply. She'd thought a part-time Devin would be better than no Devin at all. But seeing him—and not having him—caused a little slash of pain each time they met. She couldn't forget. She didn't *want* to forget, not deep down. She didn't want a man who felt obligated to her. She wanted her champion back. She wanted her Devin back. Anything less wasn't enough.

"That day at the cabin, you asked me to hear you out, and I did, remember?"

She nodded, remembering just how difficult it had been to say the words and to say goodbye.

"Now I'm asking the same of you. Hear me out. Please, just listen to what I have to say."

She went to the sofa and sank into the cushions, a relief after being on her feet most of the day combined with her churning emotions. But Devin didn't sit. He paced in front of her.

"When I read your article, Ell... No, wait," he amended, coming to a halt and standing before her. His dimple was nowhere in sight, hidden behind his serious expression. His dark gaze reached into her middle and grabbed her. This was the only man she'd ever given her body to. The man who had fathered the child inside her, the man who had the ability to turn her world upside down over and over again. She didn't care what he had to say for a fleeting, beautiful instant. She wanted to rise and simply walk into his arms, let him shelter her from the world outside and all the unknowns she now found herself faced with.

But she didn't. She had left him all those years ago because she had been afraid to rely on him too much. She'd been afraid of being overshadowed until her sense of self was eaten up by his strength. She'd been afraid of her own weakness. Going to him would be easy, but it still scared her. She had to know she was making decisions out of her own strength, not by relying on his.

"What is it?" She asked the question, remaining on the sofa, though it took a good part of her will to do so.

"What you said the night you told me about the baby. You were right. I didn't give you a chance when I got sick. I didn't fight for you. I wanted you to fight for me, and I was too proud to ask. I thought that when I was better I'd go after you, so I waited, hoping you'd come to your senses first. But then when the doctor said..." He stopped, swallowed thickly. "I only heard the hindrance, not the possibility, and I was afraid. And I hid behind it because you left without looking back and it hurt. I was wrong. You told me how you were feeling and I closed my mind to it."

Ella stared at him dumbfounded. Dev wasn't the kind to admit when he was wrong or apologize for it. And afraid? Oh, how she understood that part. Knowing he'd been afraid too touched her more deeply than she cared to admit. "What changed your mind?"

He squatted down before her, put his hands on her knees and looked up into her face. How she loved his face—the slight shadow of stubble on his chin, the way his eyes crinkled at the corners, the dip in the top of his lip. He had always been her ideal. Now, with his child growing within her, she realized he still was. There was no other man on earth she wanted to father her baby. Not just to father him or her, but to be a parent. He would be strong but kind, firm but caring. Supportive and fun. She swallowed, wanting to hope but afraid to because of what it would mean.

"*You* changed my mind. When you kept your word and when you wrote that article about Betty. It was the girl I remembered. I always wondered if she was in there somewhere, and she was. The Ella that was fair, and kind, and thought with her heart. Someone strong and sure of herself." He squeezed her knees. "I love that girl."

She blinked. He'd said "love", not "loved"... But they were over. It was for the best. She'd said it over and over...

"You love..." But she couldn't bring herself to say the rest.

"I love you, Ella. God knows, I never stopped. Why else would I have been so angry?"

"Angry?"

He reached up with one hand, tracing his thumb tenderly over one cheek. "God woman, you drive me insane. Always have. You could never have gotten to me so easily if I didn't love you so much. With or without any baby. It's always been you."

The words sank in, reached in, took hold. Suddenly the restraint she'd forced upon herself since she'd left his office burst forth, out on a gasp and a quick inhale. She was desperately trying not to cry.

He loved her. The words she'd never expected to hear him utter ever again still hummed in her ears. She'd given up all hope when he'd insisted they try again for the sake of the baby. She was so afraid of what it would mean, being with him, hoping. Wanting his heart but knowing she didn't have it. But

Devin, always sincere Devin, had said it, not once but twice.

"What took you so long?" she wailed, abashed at the emotional outburst, unable to stop it.

Devin sank to his knees and pulled her into his arms. "Pride," he admitted. "I wanted to fix everything. When you came back I wanted to fix things my way. At first I wanted to make you pay, and then I wanted you to come begging, admitting how wrong you were. But you never did, you strong, beautiful girl."

"I wanted to." She sniffled, burrowing into the warmth of his neck, closing her eyes and inhaling his scent. "I really wanted to. But I couldn't let it be on your terms. I was...I *am* so afraid of being swallowed up by you, Dev. I have felt so much at your mercy. At the mercy of my feelings for you, like my mother was for my father. It ruined her, that love. And yet all I wanted was... I wanted you to..." She halted, her throat closing over.

"You wanted me to love you?"

"Yes," she choked.

"And I wanted to fix things but I was too afraid to be vulnerable. I focused on the facts of our marriage rather than the most important thing—that you always were, and still are, the woman I loved."

"You were scared?" She couldn't believe it. Devin was never afraid. He'd fought cancer and won. He'd pulled himself up from nothing and built a successful business. He beat the odds time and again. And he'd been afraid...of her?

"My whole life I've been trying to fix things for those I care about," he said, nudging her back up on the sofa and sitting on the cushion next to her. He held her hands within his, his strong fingers cradling them possessively. "Even when we married. I loved you, but most of all I could see how you were broken and I wanted to make it better. I wanted to be your family. I thought if I could do that, it would all be okay."

"Oh, Devin," she whispered, melting a little as she realized what he'd wanted to give her.

"When Dad had his heart attack," he continued, "I built them their house so he could retire. And when Betty got sick...I wanted to fix that too. But with you and the baby... You wouldn't let me get away with that. You wouldn't let me fix anything the way I wanted. You are way too strong. Thank God."

Her heart sang at his words calling her strong. "I don't feel very strong. I was afraid to rely on you. I thought it would make me less, well, me. I jumped to conclusions. You're not the only one at fault. My letter, ending the marriage... I know now it was a call for help. I felt so lost there, so out of step with my classmates. I missed you and felt like I shouldn't. I didn't fit in and I knew I wanted to finish school. I missed you so much I felt physically ill. It scared me so much I thought walking away would be easier. I waited, remember? You didn't get the first set of divorce papers for several months. I wanted you to come back and change my mind. When you didn't... If I'd known how sick you were..."

"And I thought I had nothing to offer you at first. Then when the papers came... Oh Ell, everything I did was because I was so damn hurt."

"Do you think we can stop hurting each other?" She sniffed, pulled her fingers away to wipe beneath her eyes. Even when he'd asked to give them another shot, she'd known the gap between them was too wide. It had narrowed, but was it enough?

"It depends." He leaned forward, sitting on an angle.

"On what?"

"On whether or not you love me."

Love him? Of course she loved him. Her whole body seemed to suddenly expand with it. She slid over the few inches that remained between them, reached up with her hands and cupped his jaw.

"Of course I love you. Do you think I could have made love to you otherwise?" Emotion clogged her throat and she laughed, a thick, emotional, happy sound. "Do you think we could have made this baby without it?"

Devin closed his eyes, letting her words fill him, feeling relief that his faith—his risk—had been rewarded. More than ever he was sure they could put their marriage back together. And right now, the idea that their love—whether conscious of it or not—had made their child possible was so profound, so unbelievable, that he wanted, needed, to feel a connection.

It was more than physical. How could he have once thought it wasn't? He covered her hands with his, sliding his fingers up her arms until they caressed her neck. He felt her pulse beneath the skin, warm and strong and fast. "Ella, I..."

"Shhh," she murmured, and her fingers slid down his chin to press against his chest. "I know."

He kissed her, softly, knowing his hands trembled against her hair, her skin precious beneath the pads of his fingers. He wanted her, not only for the flare of passion between them that had never been extinguished. Right now he was as nervous as he'd been on their wedding day, when they'd been little more than kids, barely legal. Then, as now, it wasn't about bodies and desire and slaking lust. It was heart, body and soul. Taking a leap off a cliff.

"I want to see you," he whispered. He ran his fingers over her blouse and slipped the first buttons from their loops, revealing the shadows of her collarbone. "And I'm scared," he admitted. "God, that sounds ridiculous."

"Don't be scared," she whispered back. She took his hand and rose, leading him to the bedroom. He stepped inside the small room, the afternoon light filtering thinly through the slatted blinds, creating gray shadows on the wall.

Words no longer seemed to matter. As he waited, utterly helpless, Ella released the rest of her buttons, sliding the soft blouse off her shoulders and letting it drop to the floor. Her bra was white with a simple edging of lace, and she released the clasp, revealing her breasts to him. His arousal surged as he realized they were slightly fuller than before. A result of the pregnancy? So many changes going on in her body, ones he was responsible for. The thought was simply awesome. He wanted to acknowledge them, to share them with her. Holding his breath, he stepped forward and grazed his fingers over the creamy white crest on the side.

"So warm...so soft," he murmured, cupping her in his hands. Marveling at the fullness.

Between them, her fingers loosened the button on her skirt. Devin reached inside the waistband, inside her pantyhose, and pushed both down together until they lay in a heap on the carpeting. When he stood, she was before him clad only in a pair of very basic bikini panties. And with her gaze fused with his, she hooked her fingers in the band and slid them down, stepping out of them until she was completely naked.

"Now you see me," she said huskily, and he saw her nipples peak in the cool air of the room. She was beautiful. All blondness and pale, perfect skin, her dark eyes luminous in the pale light of the room. Her hands rested lightly on her pelvic bones. Inside the V formed by her fingers and thumbs, their baby was growing, this very minute.

"And you're beautiful," he answered, struggling to find the

words to express everything he was feeling and coming up short. How could he explain how much she still meant to him? How her strength was what had made this at all possible? What he was feeling was awe, pure and simple.

He ran his hand from her shoulder blade down over her bottom, adoring her skin, her scent rising in the air, a cloud of seduction weaving around them. His lips teased at the side of her mouth, tiny butterfly kisses, wanting to be gentle, slow and feeling a fire rage within him that was threatening to burn out of control. The battle, the holding back and hovering so close, was delicious.

But when she sighed blissfully against his mouth, he knew he was losing. He picked her up and carried her the few steps to the bed, laying her down on the soft duvet. And when she was stretched out before him, he felt an unfamiliar stinging behind his eyes.

Before he could do another thing, he leaned over and pressed a soft kiss to the gentle mound of her belly. It hadn't yet changed shape, he realized with wonder. But it didn't matter. His son or daughter—theirs—made with love. And if he had anything to say about it, they would come into this life the same way. Loved.

"Oh, Devin." He heard her whisper, and her hand came to rest on his head.

The warmth of her skin on his face, the blessing of her hand on his hair, the absolute acceptance... This was the sweetest moment of his life. He wanted to claim her, to love her and protect her for the rest of their lives.

He gave one more kiss and straightened, unbuttoning his shirt, shucking his trousers. He needed to feel her skin on his, needed to feel himself inside her, connected in every possible way. "Do you know how much I want you, Ella?" He knelt on the bed beside her, needing to be perfectly clear before he put his stamp of possession on her.

"I think I do," she replied, the smile sharpened by an edge of arousal. "Are you going to make me wait much longer?"

His answer was to slide within her, watch her eyelids drift closed as he moved, slowly, completely. And when her eyes opened again, nothing prepared him for the force of the connection—body, heart, soul.

It was unhurried, the way he slipped into her body, the way she gave—and took—pleasure. Sweat glistened on their skin, and still they reveled in it, until Devin could stand it no longer. He rolled over so that she was on top, and gripped her hips, surrendering to her.

"Love me, Ell."

The tips of her hair swung against her shoulders as she began rocking her hips, driving him insane with the seductive rhythm. The beats quickened, and she put her hands on the pillow beside his head, grinding against him, seeking her own release. Swept up in the wave, Devin lifted his head and caught one sweat-slicked nipple in his mouth. He felt the goosebumps erupt on her skin at the same moment she cried out, pulsing around him. He gripped harder and with one last frantic push, emptied inside her.

As the haze cleared from his eyes, he felt the warm moisture of tears on his chest.

"Hey," he murmured, tucking the waterfall of her hair over her shoulder. "Hey, don't cry. It's going to be okay."

Ella sniffled, forced herself to slide off his warm, strong body and melted against his side. Her own body felt boneless, sated and perfect. This had been more than even love today. It had been soul-deep, life altering. And that was scary as hell in its perfection.

"Your body is different, do you know that?" His voice came, rough and sexy, from the pillow beside her.

"Different how?"

"Softer somehow."

"Gee, thanks Dev." Ella felt a bubble of laughter rise up. It was hard to be offended when cuddled up to a man who had just satisfied her so utterly.

"What I mean is... Oh hell. You're the wordsmith. You're just...blooming. Glowing somehow. Whatever it is, it's sexy as hell."

"I think that was a compliment."

"Of the highest order."

"Then thank you."

Silence fell for a few minutes until they'd each caught their breath better.

"Dev?"

"Hmmm?"

Oh God, the lazy way he could hum that single syllable made her want to climb on top of him all over again. But there were more important things to do first. "What do we do now, Dev?"

"Do you still want the Boston job?"

She sat up suddenly, raised up on her elbow as she stared down at him. "What?"

"The Boston job. I asked you if you still wanted it."

He looked serious. He sounded serious. "Do you mean you'd go with me?"

"If it is what you really want."

But did she? What was in Boston? Career opportunity. But her roots were here. Devin was here, and she knew DMQ was important to him. Even mentioning sacrificing that was more than she could ask for. And he'd been right about one thing. Their child's grandparents were here, and all sorts of other people who cared about them. The cabin... More than once she'd recalled his words about it being a weekend retreat for the family. Teaching their son or daughter to fish and ride. The picture was too beautiful to erase from her mind.

"No, I don't still want the Boston job," she replied decidedly, leaning on his warm chest and resting her chin on her hands. "I thought I wanted to leave here, but what I really wanted to leave was a past that had too many hurtful reminders."

Her skin shivered. They were still naked and on top of the covers.

"Get under with me," Devin suggested, and in seconds she was under the blankets with him, curled up in his arms, their legs intertwined.

"Devin?"

"Hmmm?"

There was that syllable again. Ella would never get tired of hearing it.

"Remember the night I came back to town?"

He chuckled, the sound rumbling in his chest and warming her from the inside out. "Like I could forget."

"I paid two thousand dollars for a weekend with you."

"A fool and his money..." he teased.

"Best money I've ever spent," she retorted, giving him a jab in the ribs. He laughed, pulling her closer until a hair wouldn't have fit between them.

"Dev..." She felt a little hesitancy now. She'd been the one to insist time and time again that he give her a divorce. Now to be swinging so far the other direction... But she loved him. She didn't want to go on without him.

"Devin…"

"What, honey?"

She rose up now, tucking her hair behind her ears. She took a big breath, gathering her courage.

"What am I bid for more than a weekend with me…and our baby…" She beseeched his eyes, suddenly so nervous, so afraid and needing him to understand what she was asking. "For maybe a lot longer than a weekend."

He laughed then, a big, glorious laugh as he pulled her back down on the mattress. "Lord, I love you, Ella. I don't want to fix what was wrong between us. I want to start over, the right way." He kissed the tip of her nose, looked into her eyes, his own alight with mischief. "What am I bid, you ask? Only everything I am, and everything I have. Would that be enough?"

"If only Scooter Brown were here with his gavel."

"He'd be getting an eyeful. What's the verdict?"

"Going once…" She slid her hand up his calf.

"Going twice?" he asked, running his fingers over her shoulder.

"Sold," she whispered, reaching for his hand and covering her heart, "to the highest bidder."

Epilogue

The bell over the door tinkled as another customer came in. Ella looked up at Devin with a wide smile. The bell had been tinkling non-stop since one o'clock—the moment she'd sat in a chair and started signing copies of her first novel.

"Ella, honey, you need a cup of tea or water or anything?" Betty Tucker, fully recovered and back to her old self with a full head of hair—it had come in dark brown—touched Ella's elbow. During the months of Betty's recovery, Ella had seen the older woman exhibit a strength of spirit that was so inspiring. Many times Ella or Devin had sat by her bedside as the chemo raged away at the cancer, had laughed as they'd picked out scarves and hats and had cheered with her when the first scan came back clean, only weeks before Jackson's birth. Ella had dedicated the book to Betty, for without her their reunion never would have taken place at all.

"No thanks, Betty, I'm fine." She smiled up into Betty's face, seeing a woman who had become not only a friend but a mother and honorary grandparent to her baby. "But thank you. The whole afternoon has been wonderful." She paused to sign a book and speak to the reader before turning back to Betty. "You've done a great job with The Nook. Dev's business sense was right on the money. As usual."

"Best job I ever had," Betty replied with a lightning grin.

"The boss is tolerable too." She threw a wink at Devin, who was standing beside a stroller with a wide canopy. Ella signed another book, handing it to an enthusiastic customer and soaking in the sweetness of the moment.

Rather than the freelancing she'd planned, Devin had encouraged her to write a book like she'd always wanted—right after they'd taken care of the tiny detail of getting married again—this time for good. She'd still been pregnant when she'd sent the manuscript off to an agent with a wing and a prayer, never expecting her first attempt would sell but obscenely pleased with herself for accomplishing it. Now here she was, home in Durango, signing copies with her husband and their one-year-old son by her side.

Incredible.

Jackson woke from his stroller nap with a bad-natured fuss, and Ella moved to unstrap him. "I've got it," Devin said, staying her hands with his and placing a light kiss on her lips. "Today's your day. I get diaper duty while you get to be glamorous."

When he returned, Betty had brought Ella juice and she was chatting to a couple of old school friends that she and Devin had double dated with.

"Devin, you remember Steve and Daphne."

"Sure I do." He shook hands with both of them, while Jackson sat on his left arm and played with the collar of his shirt. "You're working construction now, aren't you, Steve? For old man Durst."

"That's right." Steve, six foot three and brawny, gave a nod.

"We were just saying how crazy it is that all four of us are back in town and still together, you know?"

"It's crazy all right," Devin replied. Jackson reached for Ella, so she took him from Devin's arms and gave him a bounce. Ella smiled at Daphne, still so very cute in snug jeans and a pink T-shirt. "Have you got any kids?"

"Not yet," Steve answered, and Ella dropped the subject at the way Daphne averted her eyes. A thin line of tension seemed to appear between the couple. Not long afterwards, Steve and Daphne departed.

The afternoon was winding down and Ella was down to only a handful of books when Devin and Jackson snuck up behind her again. "Did you have a good afternoon?"

She beamed up at him. "The best."

"The best?" He emphasized the word, giving her a suggestive look. His dimple popped when her cheeks started to heat. He could still do that, even now.

"Well, maybe not the best, but definitely up there. Top five for sure."

Betty was ringing off the till and Jackson was sucking on an animal cracker. To Ella, it was perfect.

"Then shall we go home, Mrs. McQuade?"

"Oh, I think so," she replied, sneaking her arm around his waist and squeezing. "This wife has had enough glamour for one afternoon."

They were almost to the car when she put a finger to her lips. "Tell me, Devin, which would you like first? A new book, or a new baby?"

He looked down at the stroller, and back up at Ella, his eyes begging the question. With a joyous laugh, she leaned up on tiptoe to give him a kiss before getting into the car.

About the Author

To learn more about Donna Alward, please visit
www.donnaalward.com, check out her blog at
www.donnaalward.blogspot.com, or join her newsletter. Send
an email to Donna at donnaalward@hotmail.com.

Indianapolis
Marion County
Public Library

Renew by Phone
269-5222

Renew on the Web
www.imcpl.org

For General Library Information
please call 269-1700

DEMCO

LaVergne, TN USA
17 March 2011

220596LV00002B/144/P

9 781609 280185